MARVEL ACTION
SPIDER-MAN
BAD LUCK

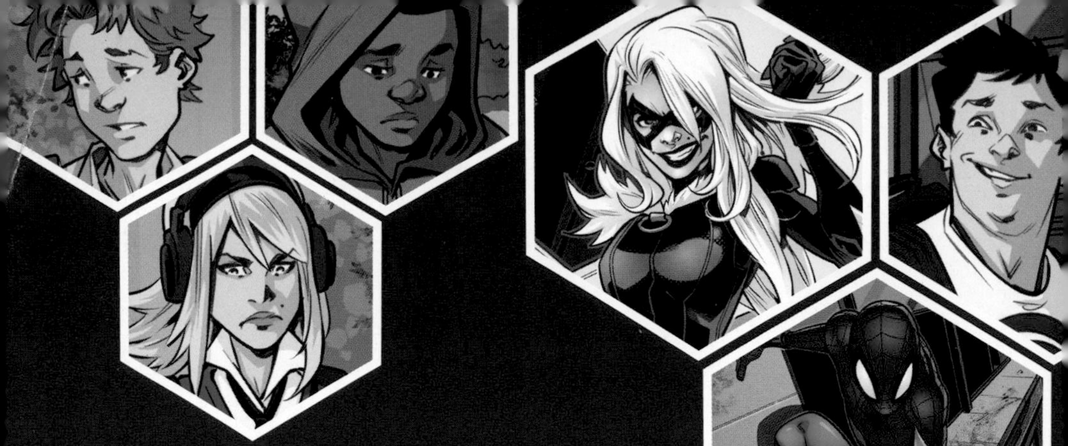
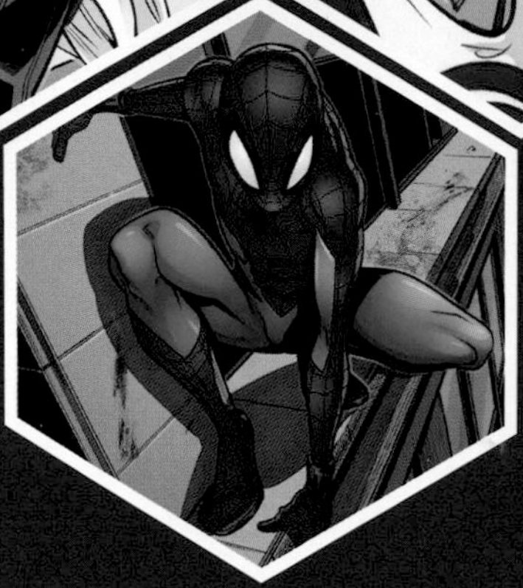

Marvel Publishing:

Jeff Youngquist: VP Production & Special Projects
Caitlin O'Connell: Assistant Editor, Special Projects
Sven Larsen: Director, Licensed Publishing
David Gabriel: SVP Print, Sales & Marketing
C.B. Cebulski: Editor-In-Chief
Joe Quesada: Chief Creative Officer
Dan Buckley: President, Marvel Entertainment
Alan Fine: Executive Producer

IDW Publishing:

IDW

Chris Ryall, President & Publisher/CCO
Cara Morrison, Chief Financial Officer
Matthew Ruzicka, Chief Accounting Officer
David Hedgecock, Associate Publisher
John Barber, Editor-in-Chief
Justin Eisinger, Editorial Director, Graphic Novels and Collections
Jerry Bennington, VP of New Product Development
Lorelei Bunjes, VP of Technology & Information Services
Jud Meyers, Sales Director
Anna Morrow, Marketing Director
Tara McCrillis, Director of Design & Production
Mike Ford, Director of Operations
Rebekah Cahalin, General Manager

Ted Adams and Robbie Robbins, IDW Founders

Cover Art by
FICO OSSIO

Cover Colors by
RONDA PATTISON

Collection Edits by
JUSTIN EISINGER
and ALONZO SIMON

Production Assistance by
CLAUDIA CHONG

ISBN: 978-1-68405-562-3 23 22 21 20 1 2 3 4

Special thanks: **Nick Lowe**

Originally published as MARVEL ACTION: SPIDER-MAN issues #7-9.

For international rights, contact licensing@idwpublishing.com

MARVEL

MARVEL ACTION SPIDER-MAN

BAD LUCK

WRITTEN BY DELILAH S. DAWSON

ART BY FICO OSSIO

COLORS BY RONDA PATTISON

LETTERS BY SHAWN LEE

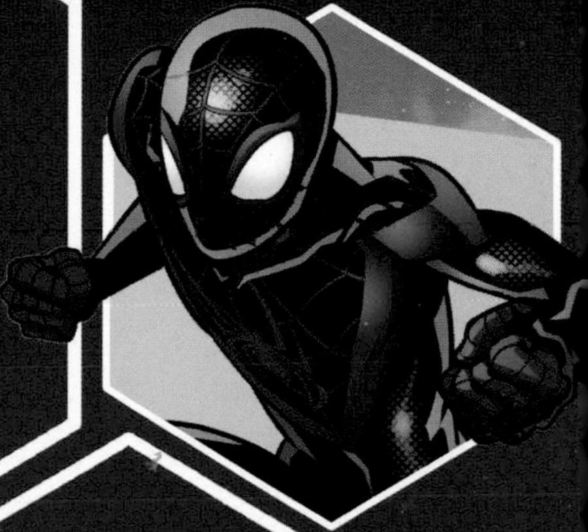

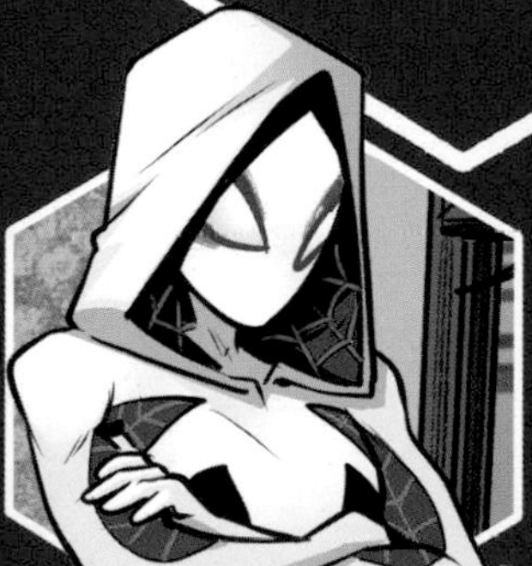

ASSISTANT EDITOR ANNI PERHEENTUPA

ASSOCIATE EDITORS ELIZABETH BREI & CHASE MAROTZ

EDITOR DENTON J. TIPTON

EDITOR-IN-CHIEF JOHN BARBER

SPIDER-MAN CREATED BY STAN LEE & STEVE DITKO

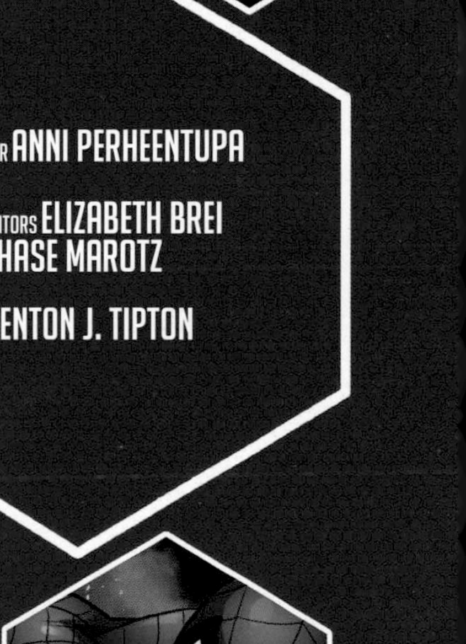

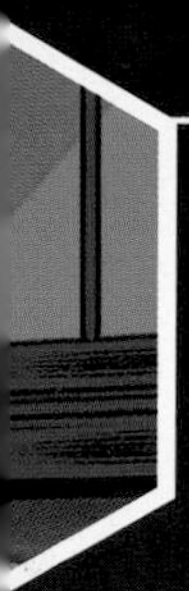

ART BY: FICO OSSIO
COLORS BY: RONDA PATTISON

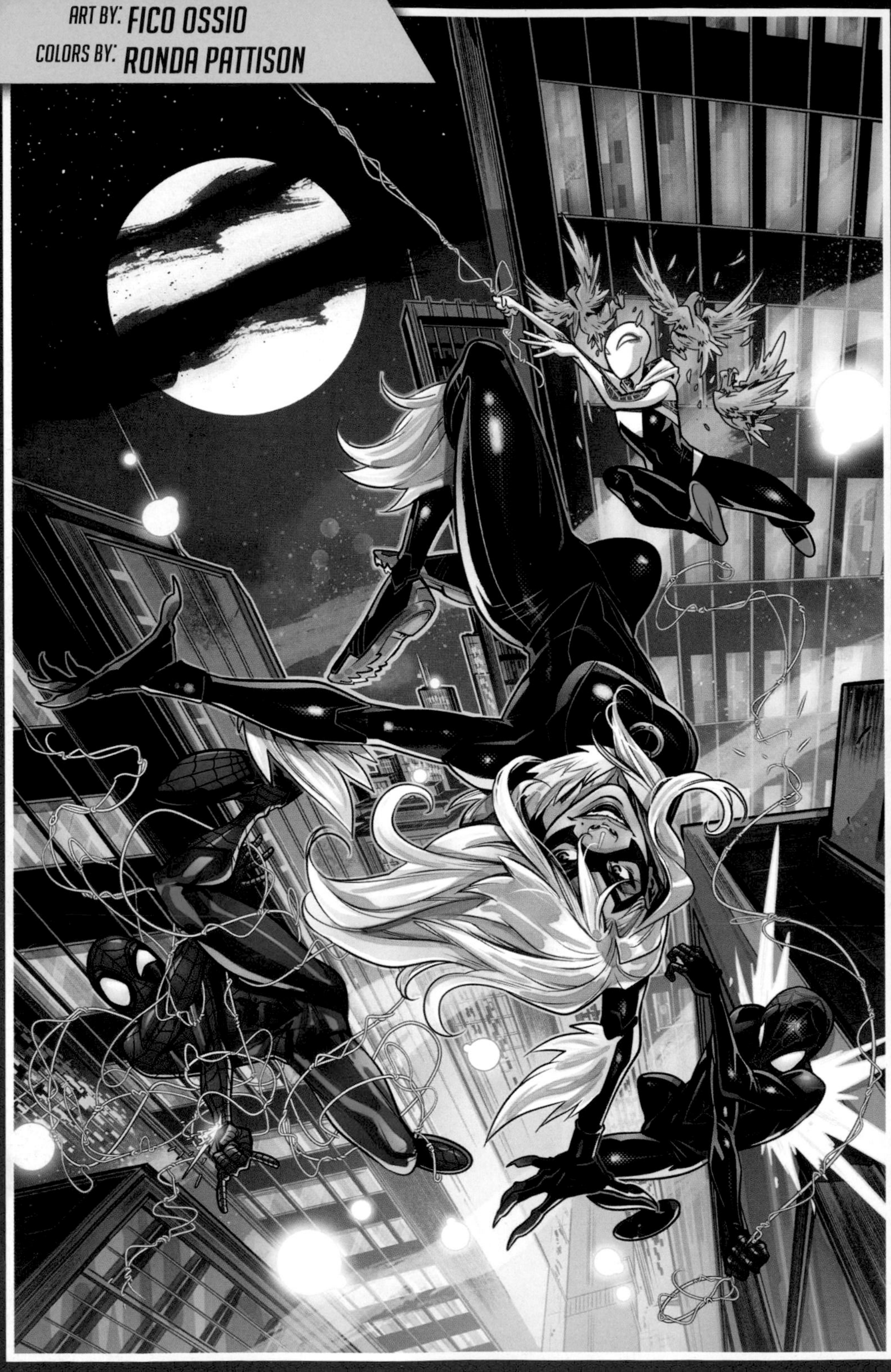

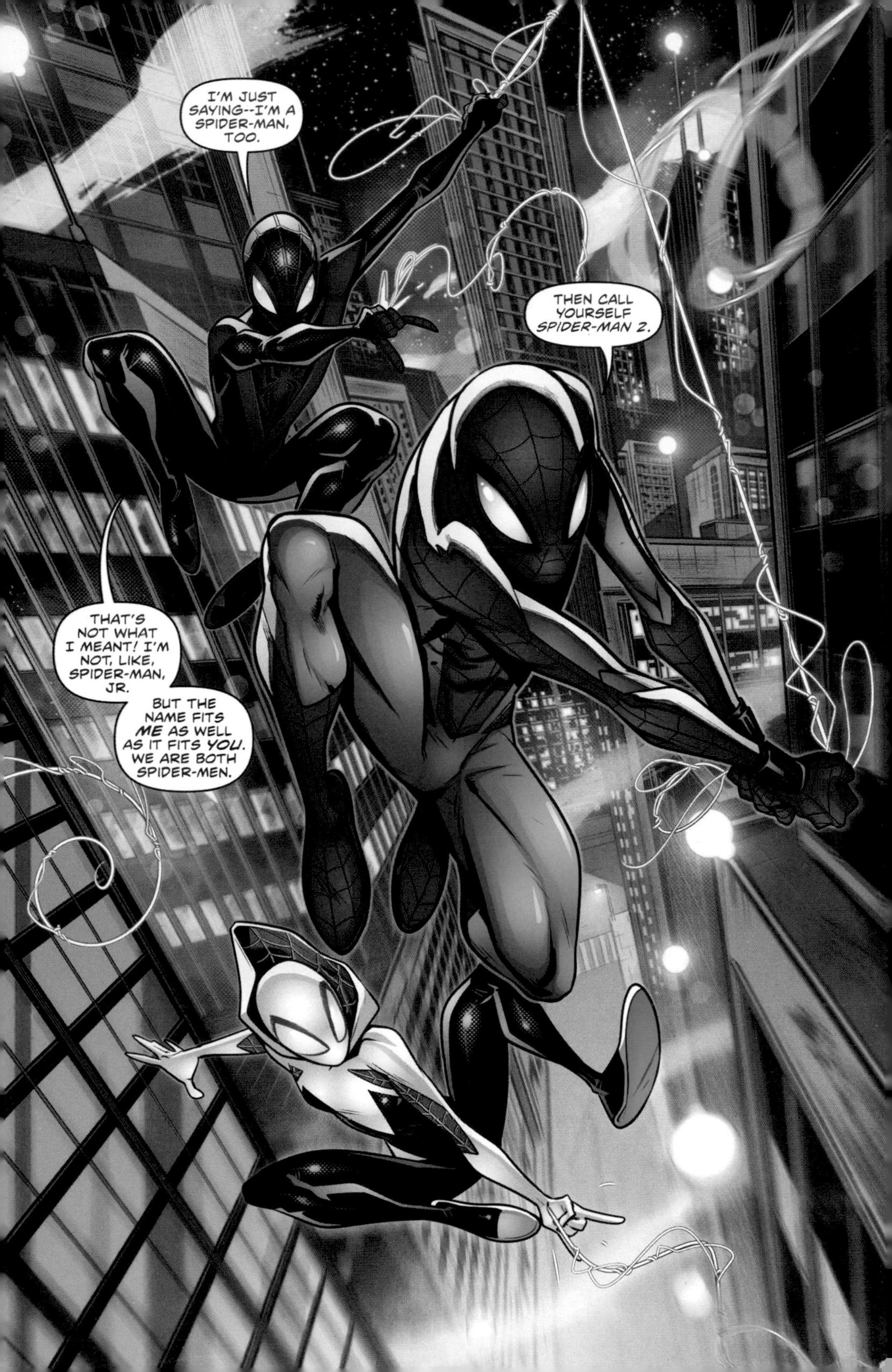
I'M JUST SAYING--I'M A SPIDER-MAN, TOO.
THEN CALL YOURSELF SPIDER-MAN 2.
THAT'S NOT WHAT I MEANT! I'M NOT, LIKE, SPIDER-MAN, JR.
BUT THE NAME FITS ME AS WELL AS IT FITS YOU. WE ARE BOTH SPIDER-MEN.

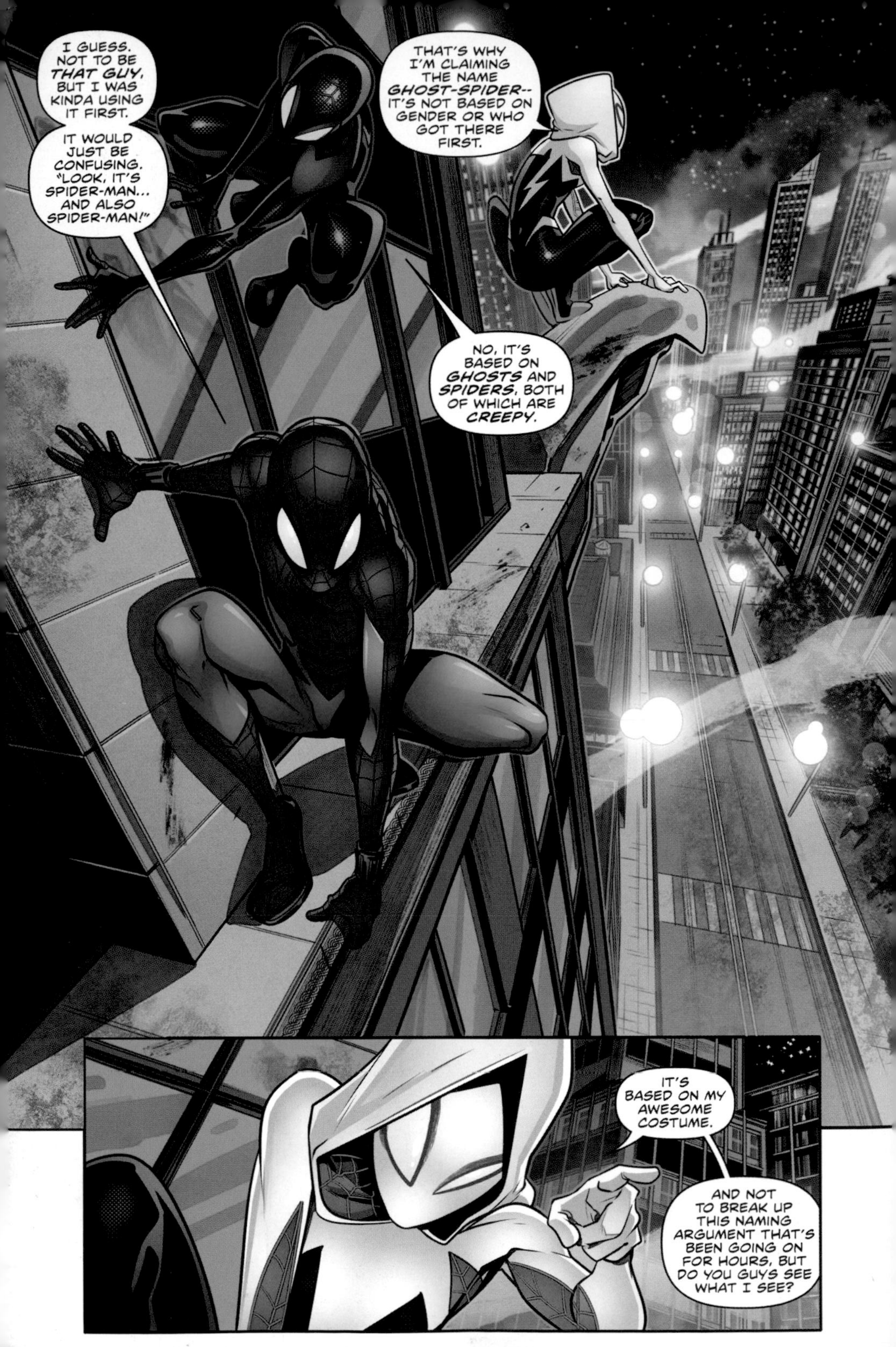
I GUESS. NOT TO BE THAT GUY, BUT I WAS KINDA USING IT FIRST.
IT WOULD JUST BE CONFUSING. "LOOK, IT'S SPIDER-MAN... AND ALSO SPIDER-MAN!"
THAT'S WHY I'M CLAIMING THE NAME GHOST-SPIDER-- IT'S NOT BASED ON GENDER OR WHO GOT THERE FIRST.
NO, IT'S BASED ON GHOSTS AND SPIDERS, BOTH OF WHICH ARE CREEPY.
IT'S BASED ON MY AWESOME COSTUME.
AND NOT TO BREAK UP THIS NAMING ARGUMENT THAT'S BEEN GOING ON FOR HOURS, BUT DO YOU GUYS SEE WHAT I SEE?

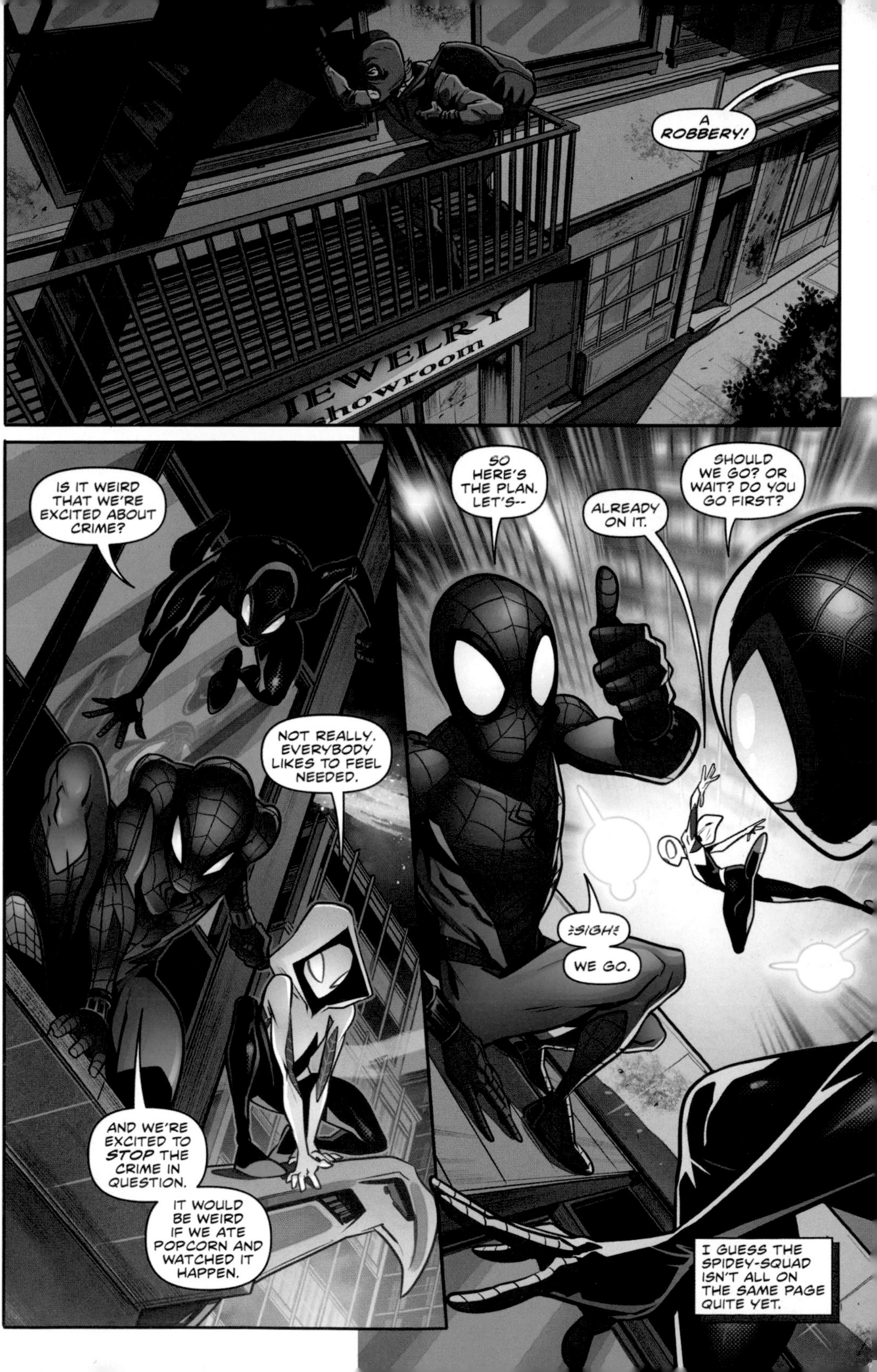
A ROBBERY!
JEWELRY
showroom
IS IT WEIRD THAT WE'RE EXCITED ABOUT CRIME?
NOT REALLY. EVERYBODY LIKES TO FEEL NEEDED.
AND WE'RE EXCITED TO *STOP* THE CRIME IN QUESTION.
IT WOULD BE WEIRD IF WE ATE POPCORN AND WATCHED IT HAPPEN.
SO HERE'S THE PLAN. LET'S--
ALREADY ON IT.
SHOULD WE GO? OR WAIT? DO YOU GO FIRST?
SIGH
WE GO.
I GUESS THE SPIDEY-SQUAD ISN'T ALL ON THE SAME PAGE QUITE YET.

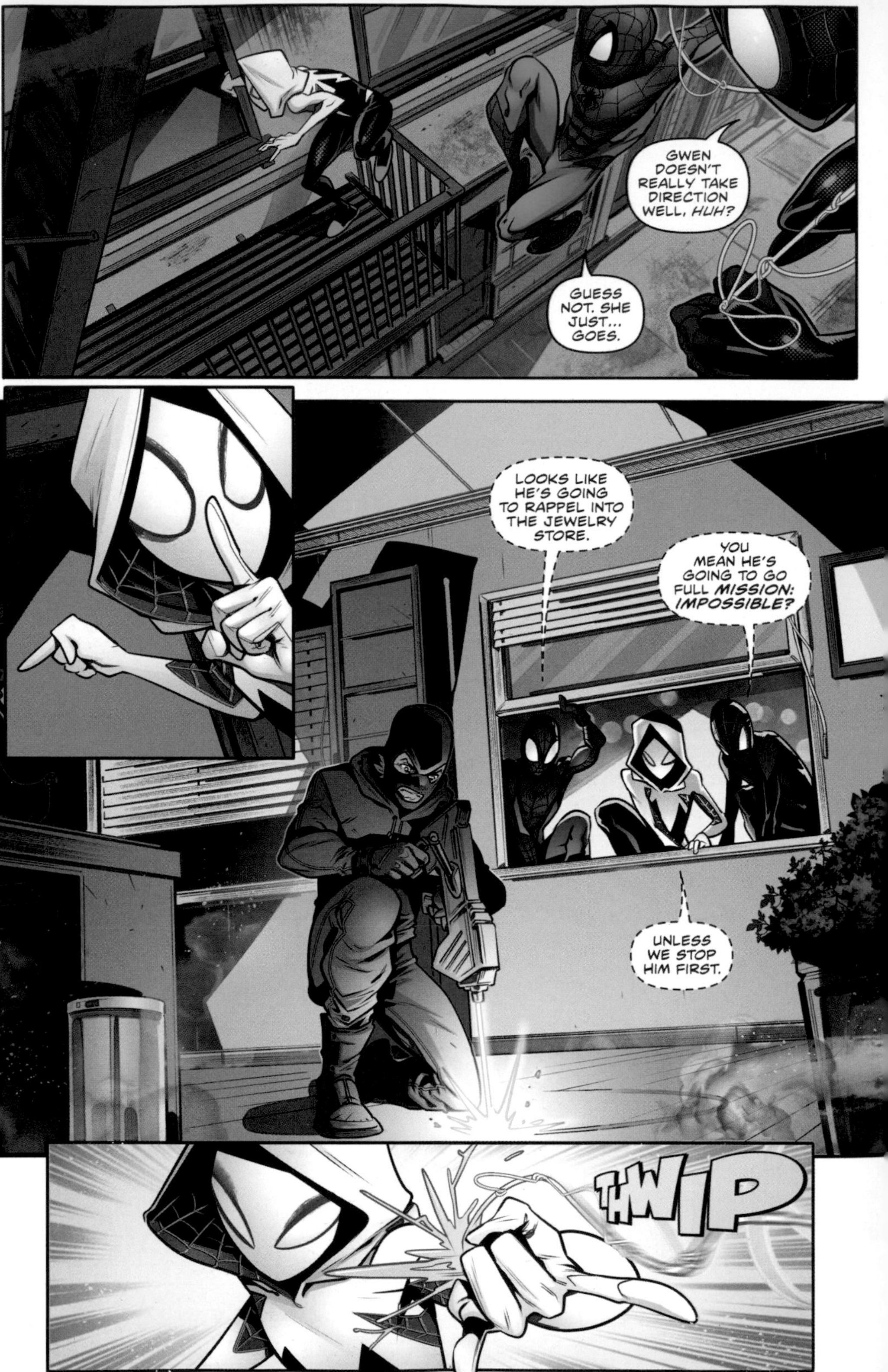
GWEN DOESN'T REALLY TAKE DIRECTION WELL, *HUH?*
GUESS NOT. SHE JUST... GOES.
LOOKS LIKE HE'S GOING TO RAPPEL INTO THE JEWELRY STORE.
YOU MEAN HE'S GOING TO GO FULL ***MISSION: IMPOSSIBLE?***
UNLESS WE STOP HIM FIRST.
THWIP

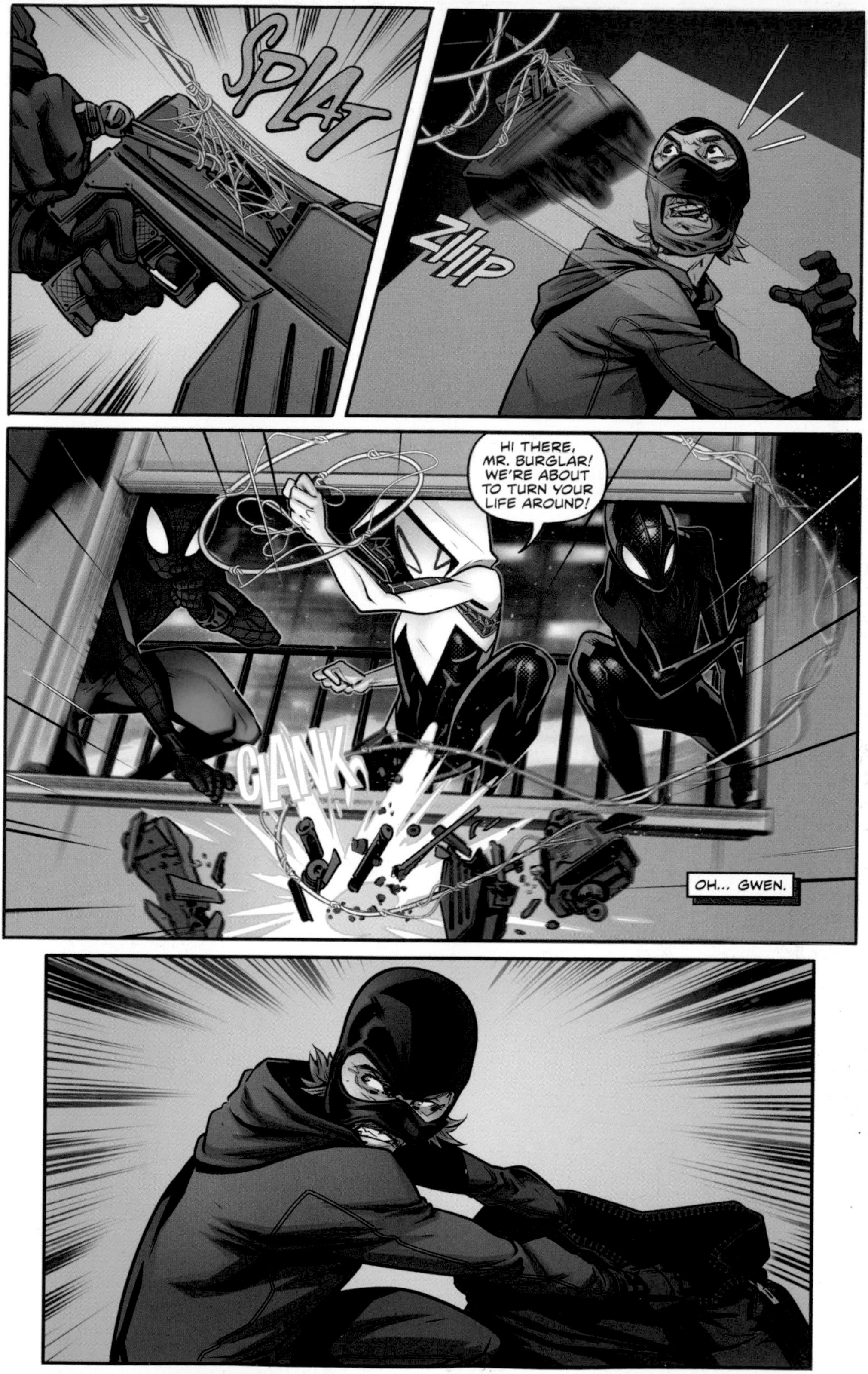
SPLAT
ZIIIP
HI THERE, MR. BURGLAR! WE'RE ABOUT TO TURN YOUR LIFE AROUND!
CLANK
OH... GWEN.

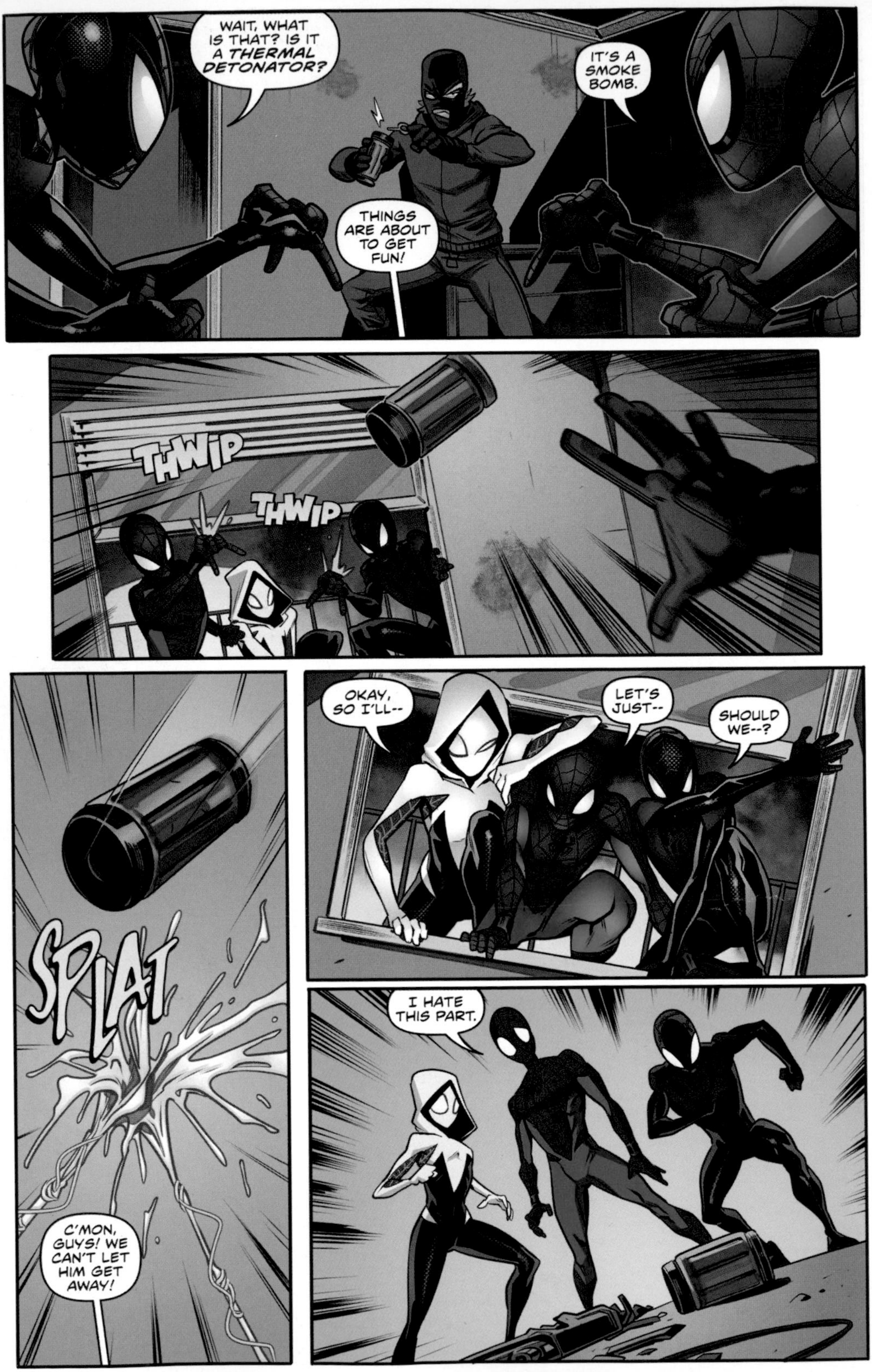
WAIT, WHAT IS THAT? IS IT A *THERMAL DETONATOR?*
IT'S A SMOKE BOMB.
THINGS ARE ABOUT TO GET FUN!
THWIP
THWIP
SPLAT
C'MON, GUYS! WE CAN'T LET HIM GET AWAY!
OKAY, SO I'LL--
LET'S JUST--
SHOULD WE--?
I HATE THIS PART.

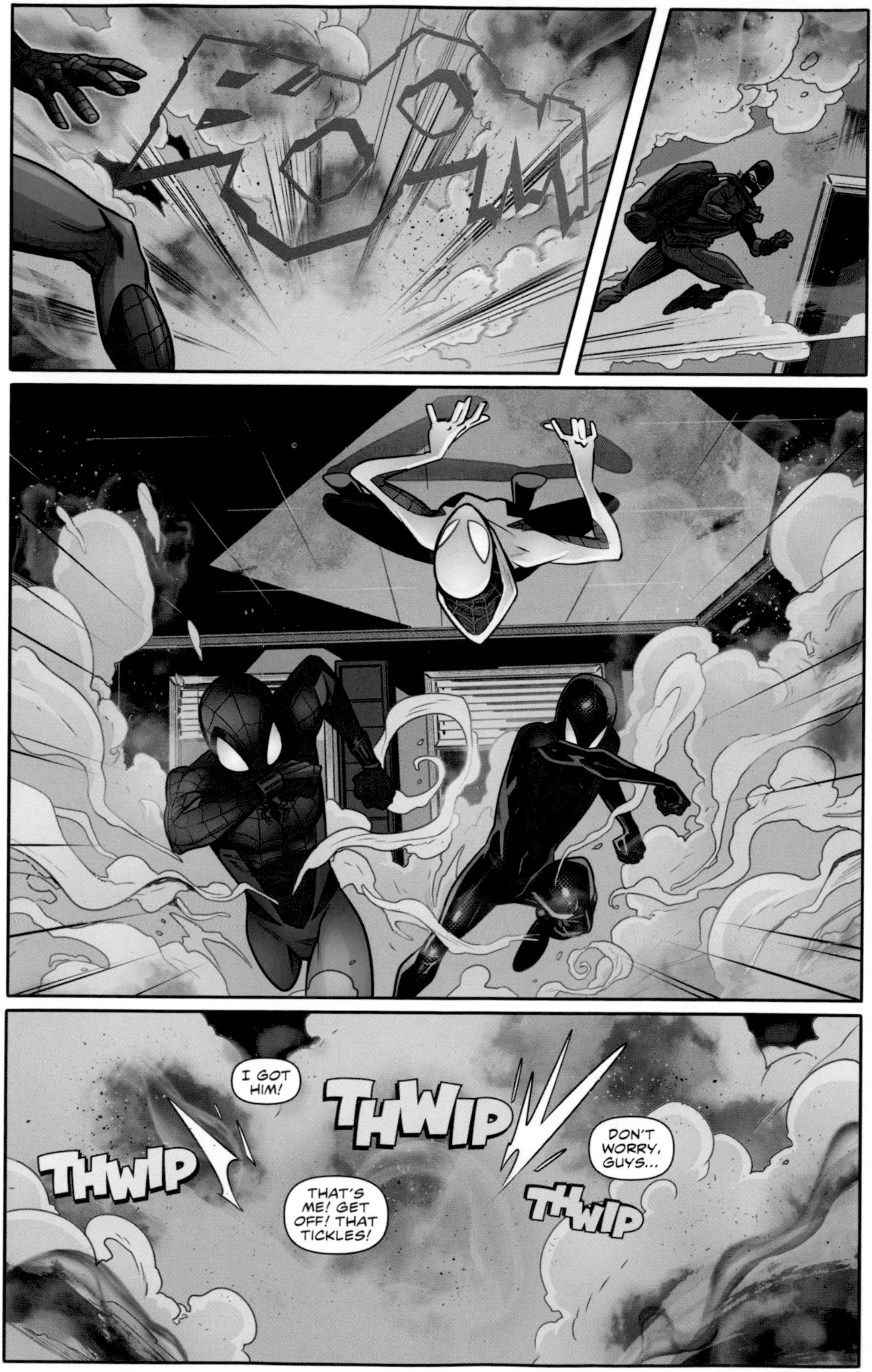
BOOM
I GOT HIM!
THWIP
THWIP
DON'T WORRY, GUYS...
THAT'S ME! GET OFF! THAT TICKLES!
THWIP

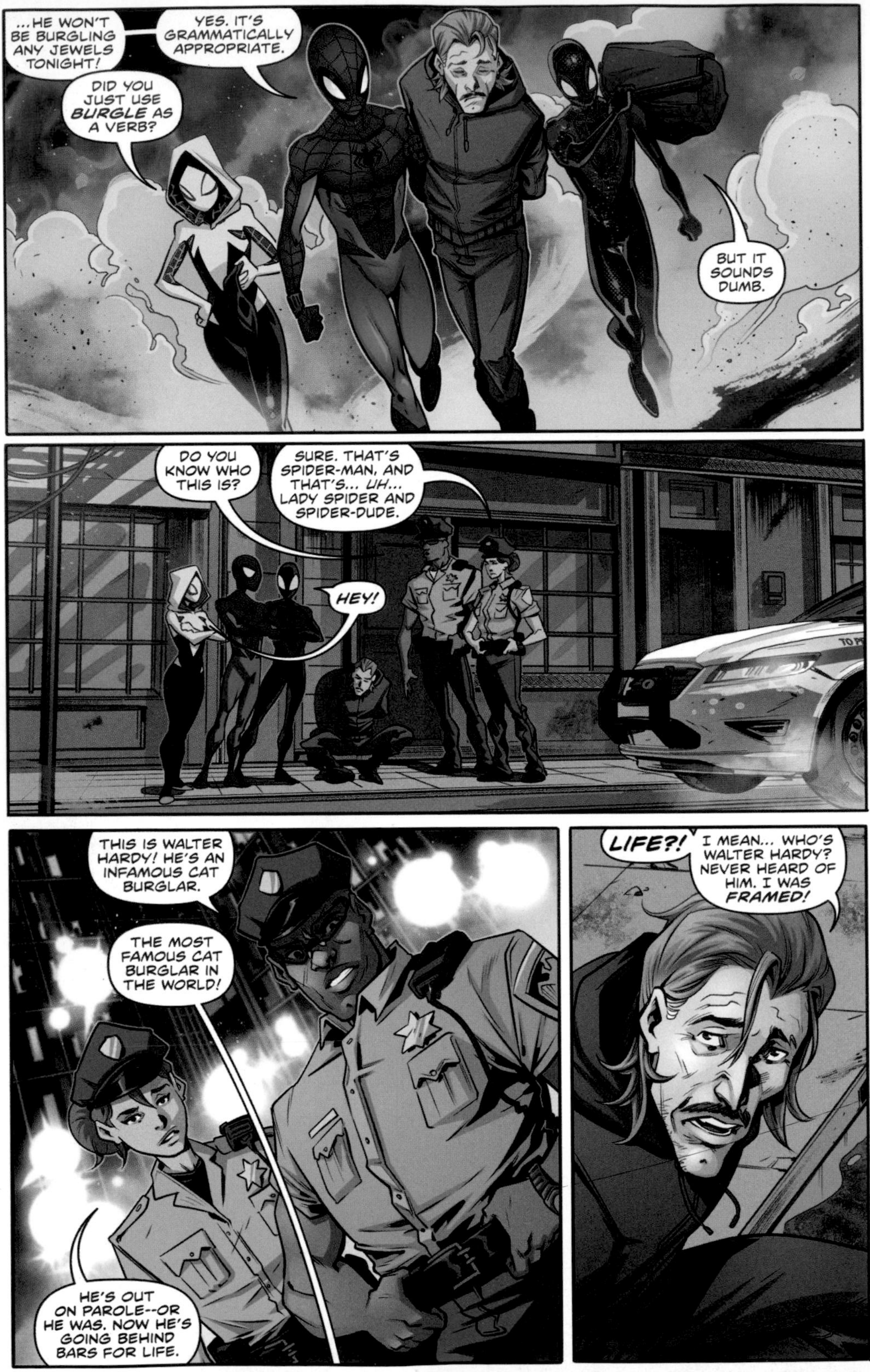
...HE WON'T BE BURGLING ANY JEWELS TONIGHT!
DID YOU JUST USE BURGLE AS A VERB?
YES. IT'S GRAMMATICALLY APPROPRIATE.
BUT IT SOUNDS DUMB.
DO YOU KNOW WHO THIS IS?
SURE. THAT'S SPIDER-MAN, AND THAT'S... UH... LADY SPIDER AND SPIDER-DUDE.
HEY!
THIS IS WALTER HARDY! HE'S AN INFAMOUS CAT BURGLAR.
THE MOST FAMOUS CAT BURGLAR IN THE WORLD!
HE'S OUT ON PAROLE--OR HE WAS. NOW HE'S GOING BEHIND BARS FOR LIFE.
LIFE?!
I MEAN... WHO'S WALTER HARDY? NEVER HEARD OF HIM. I WAS FRAMED!

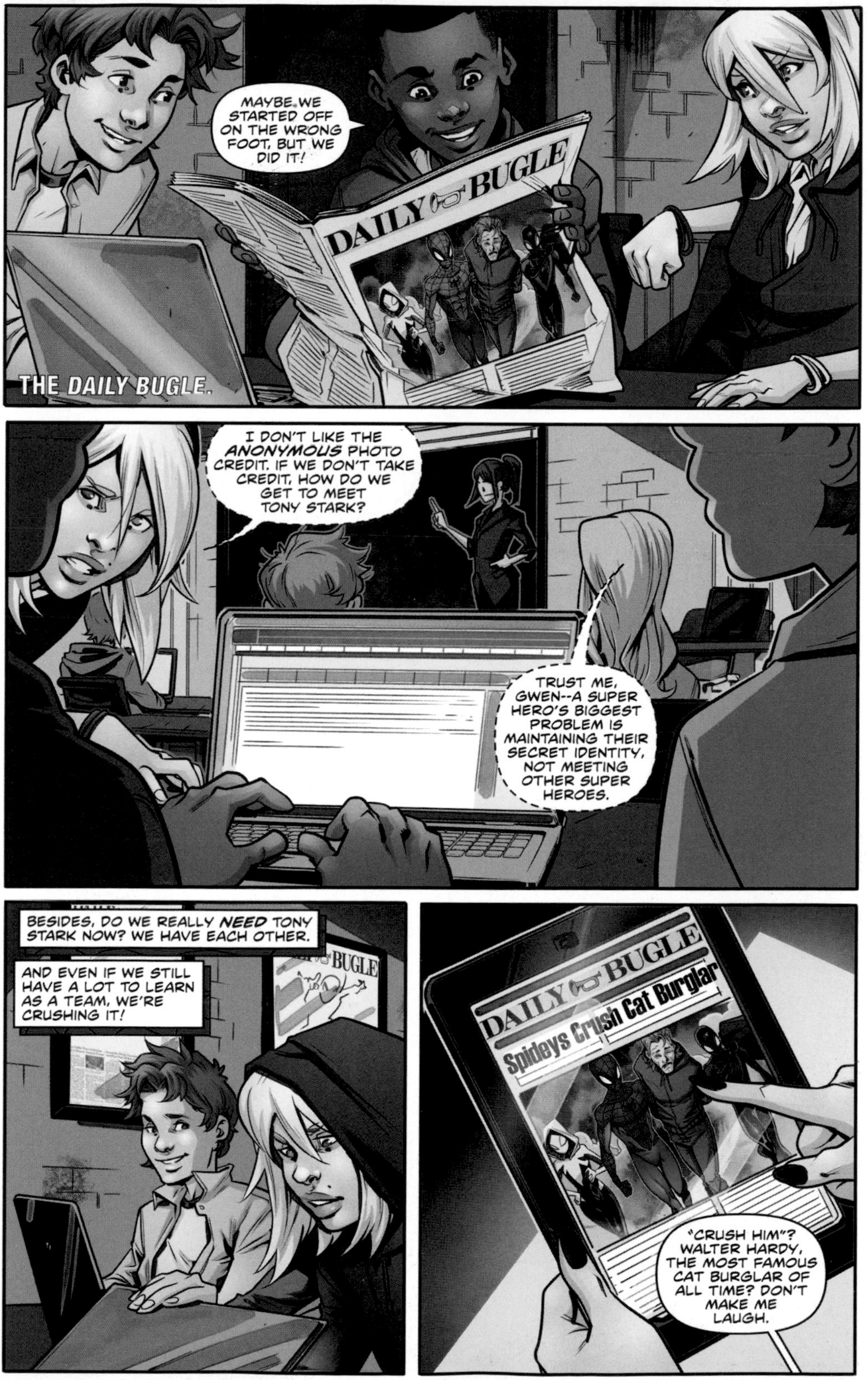
MAYBE WE STARTED OFF ON THE WRONG FOOT, BUT WE DID IT!
DAILY BUGLE
THE DAILY BUGLE.
I DON'T LIKE THE ANONYMOUS PHOTO CREDIT. IF WE DON'T TAKE CREDIT, HOW DO WE GET TO MEET TONY STARK?
TRUST ME, GWEN--A SUPER HERO'S BIGGEST PROBLEM IS MAINTAINING THEIR SECRET IDENTITY, NOT MEETING OTHER SUPER HEROES.
BESIDES, DO WE REALLY NEED TONY STARK NOW? WE HAVE EACH OTHER.
AND EVEN IF WE STILL HAVE A LOT TO LEARN AS A TEAM, WE'RE CRUSHING IT!
DAILY BUGLE
Spideys Crush Cat Burglar
"CRUSH HIM"? WALTER HARDY, THE MOST FAMOUS CAT BURGLAR OF ALL TIME? DON'T MAKE ME LAUGH.

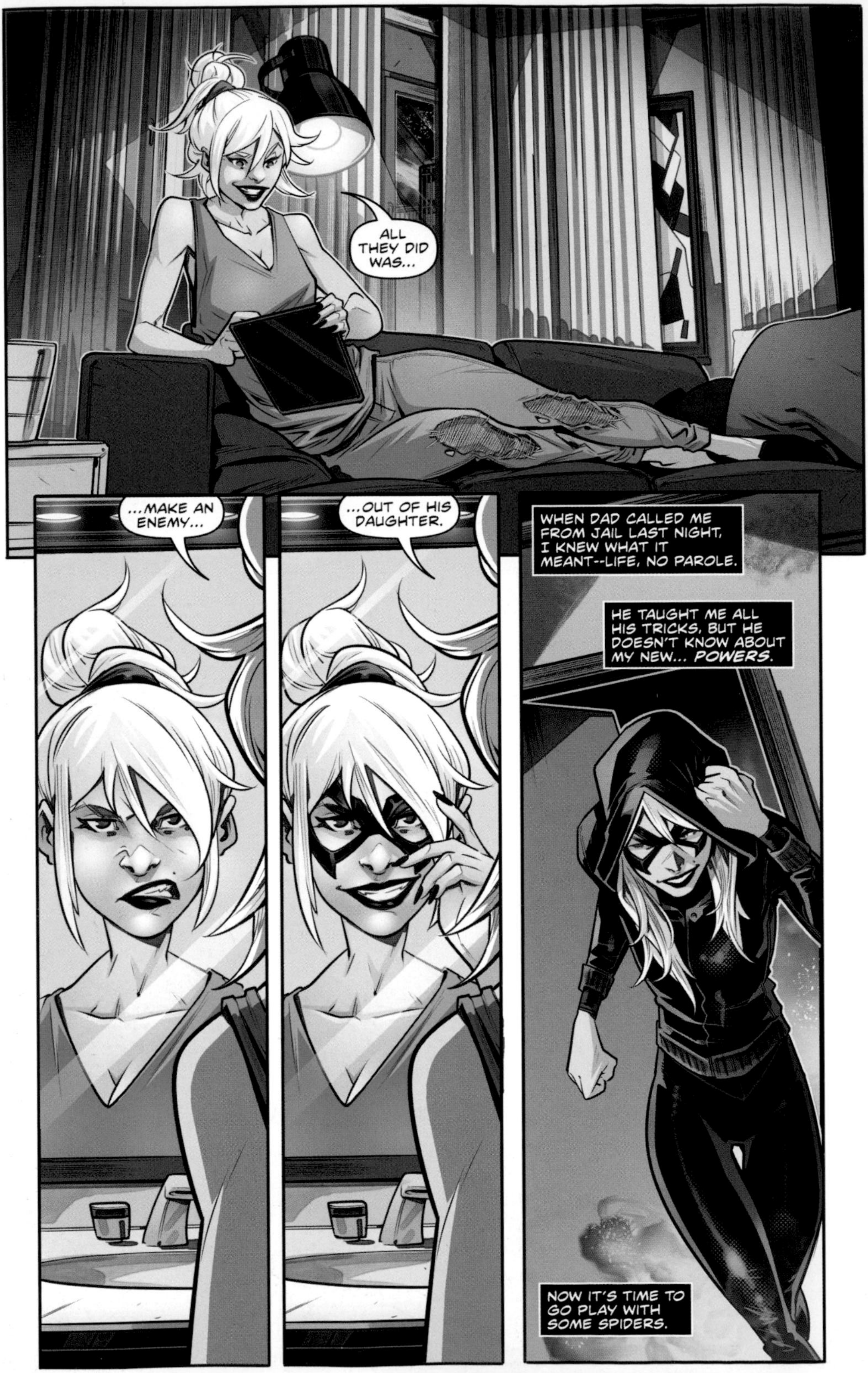
ALL THEY DID WAS...
...MAKE AN ENEMY...
...OUT OF HIS DAUGHTER.
WHEN DAD CALLED ME FROM JAIL LAST NIGHT, I KNEW WHAT IT MEANT--LIFE, NO PAROLE.
HE TAUGHT ME ALL HIS TRICKS, BUT HE DOESN'T KNOW ABOUT MY NEW... *POWERS*.
NOW IT'S TIME TO GO PLAY WITH SOME SPIDERS.

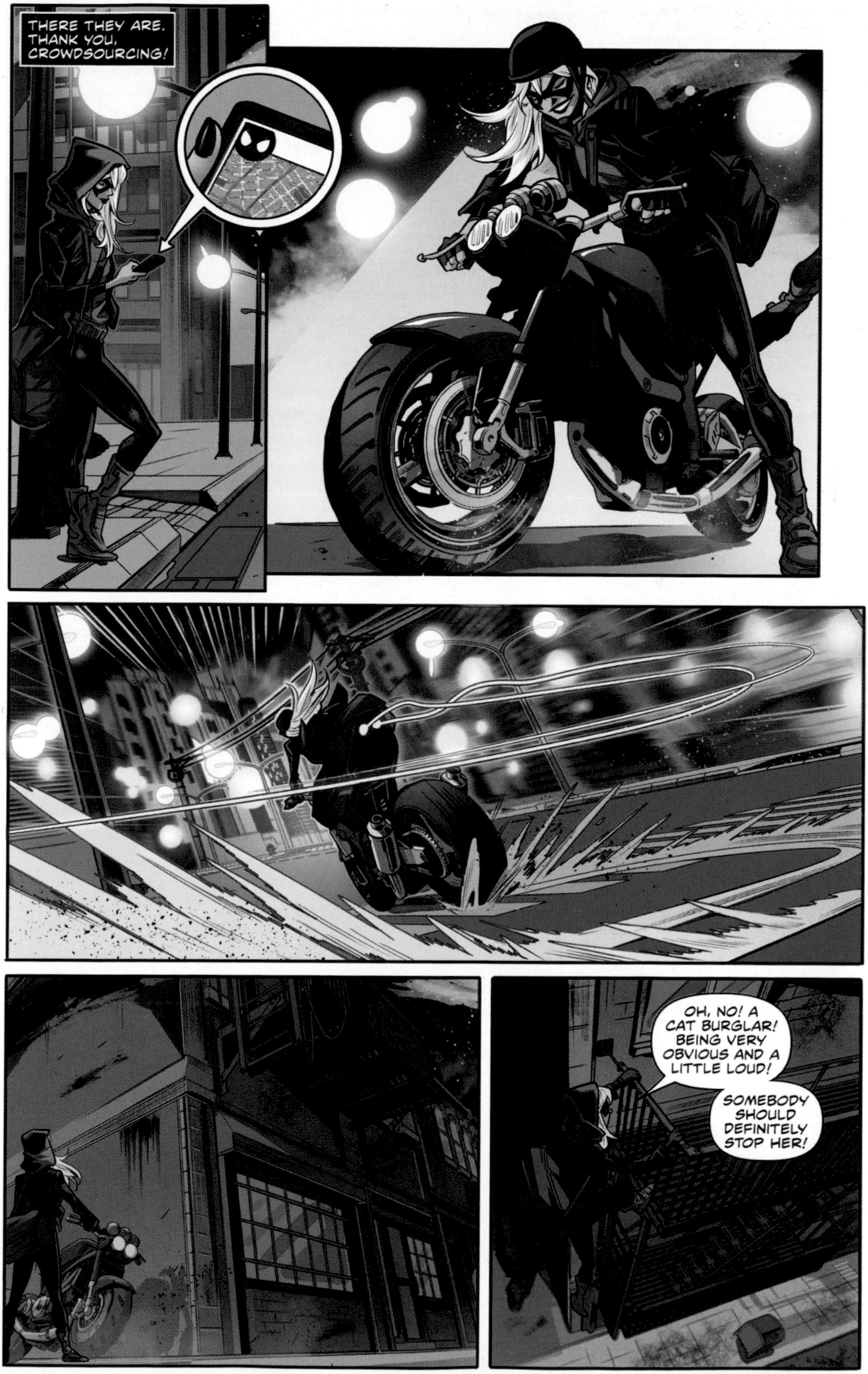
THERE THEY ARE. THANK YOU, CROWDSOURCING!
OH, NO! A CAT BURGLAR! BEING VERY OBVIOUS AND A LITTLE LOUD!
SOMEBODY SHOULD DEFINITELY STOP HER!

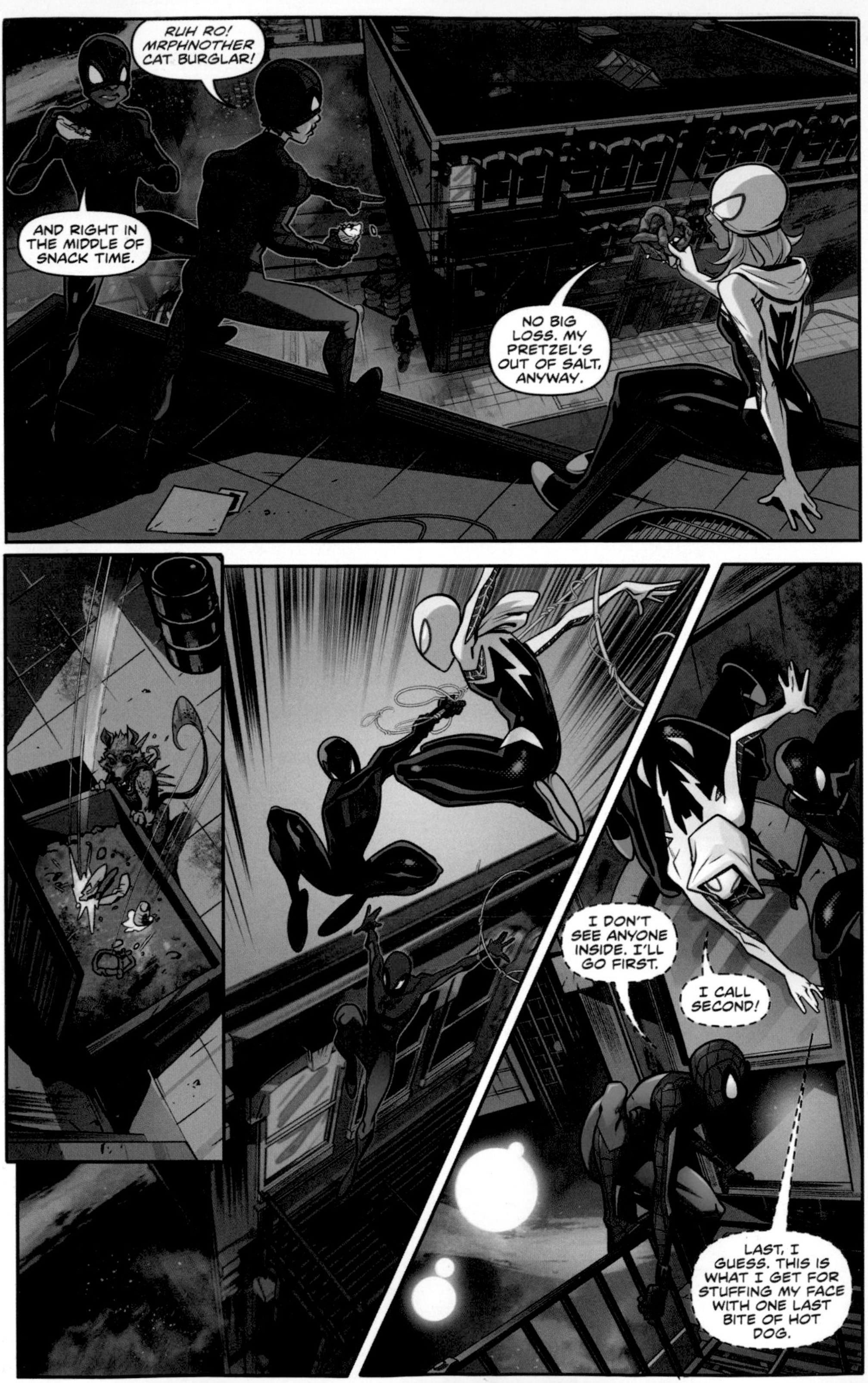
RUH RO! MRPHNOTHER CAT BURGLAR!
AND RIGHT IN THE MIDDLE OF SNACK TIME.
NO BIG LOSS. MY PRETZEL'S OUT OF SALT, ANYWAY.
I DON'T SEE ANYONE INSIDE. I'LL GO FIRST.
I CALL SECOND!
LAST, I GUESS. THIS IS WHAT I GET FOR STUFFING MY FACE WITH ONE LAST BITE OF HOT DOG.

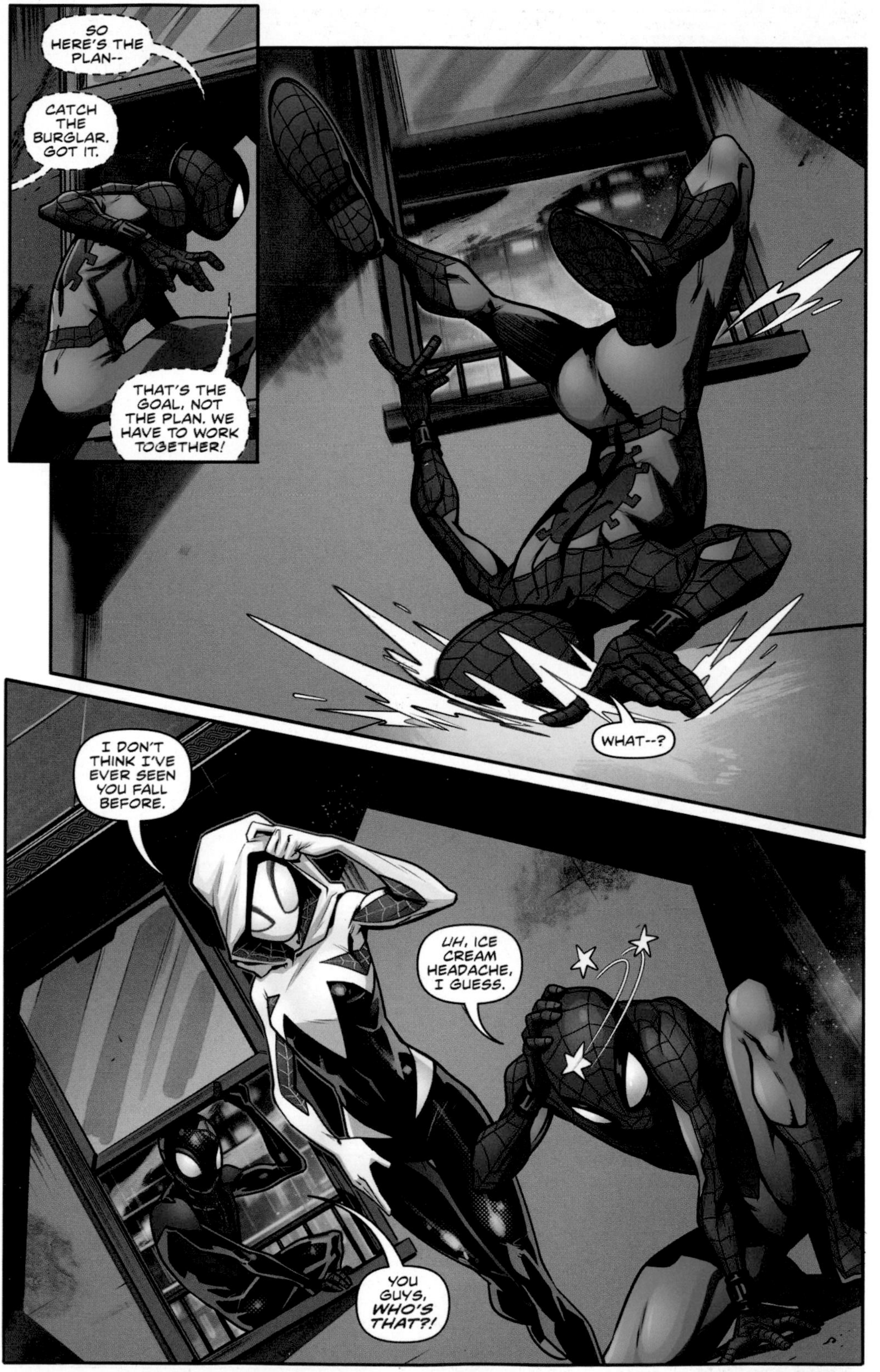

SO HERE'S THE PLAN--
CATCH THE BURGLAR. GOT IT.
THAT'S THE GOAL, NOT THE PLAN. WE HAVE TO WORK TOGETHER!
WHAT--?
I DON'T THINK I'VE EVER SEEN YOU FALL BEFORE.
UH, ICE CREAM HEADACHE, I GUESS.
YOU GUYS, WHO'S THAT?!

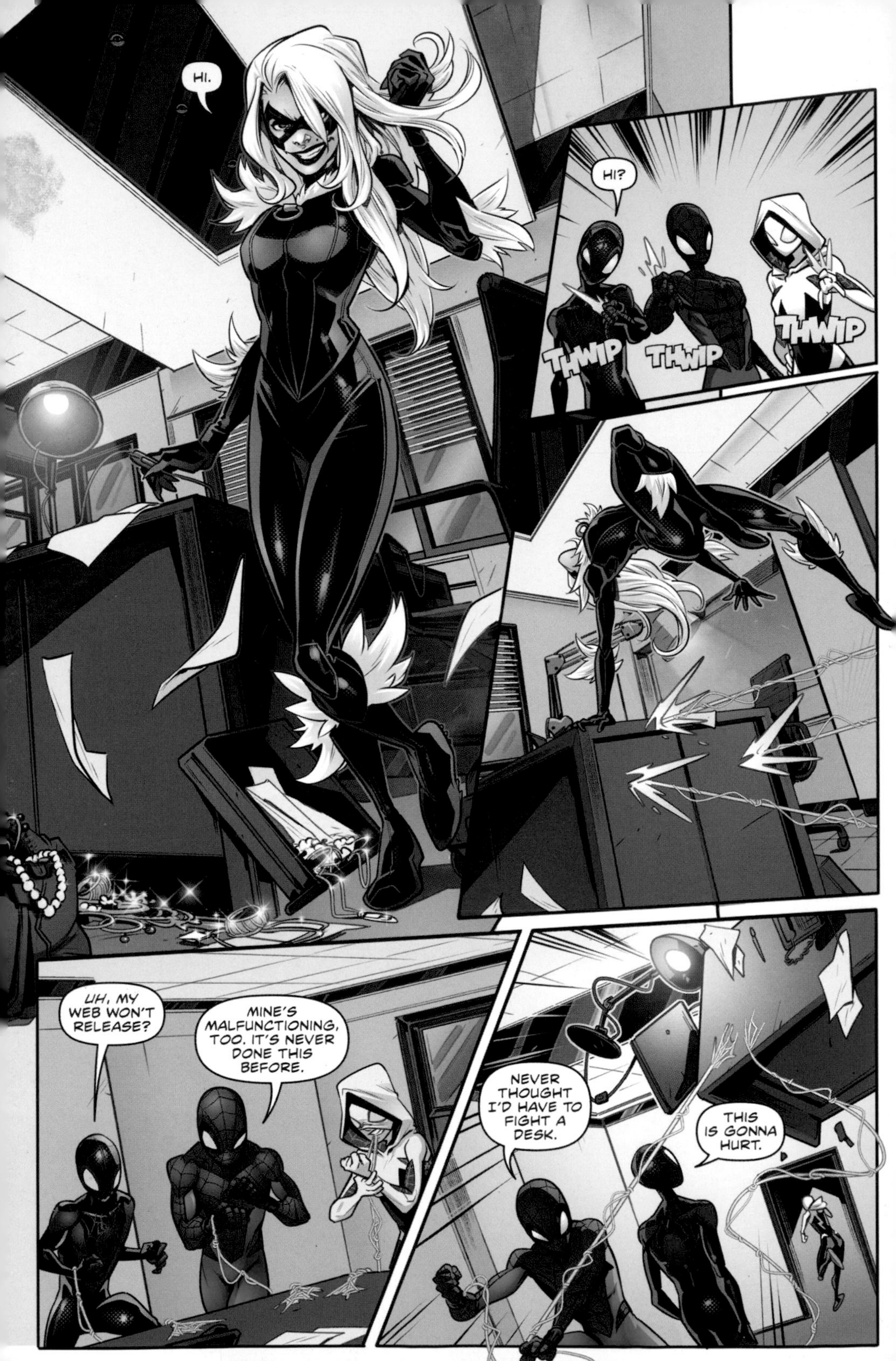
HI.
HI?
THWIP
THWIP
THWIP
UH, MY WEB WON'T RELEASE?
MINE'S MALFUNCTIONING, TOO. IT'S NEVER DONE THIS BEFORE.
NEVER THOUGHT I'D HAVE TO FIGHT A DESK.
THIS IS GONNA HURT.

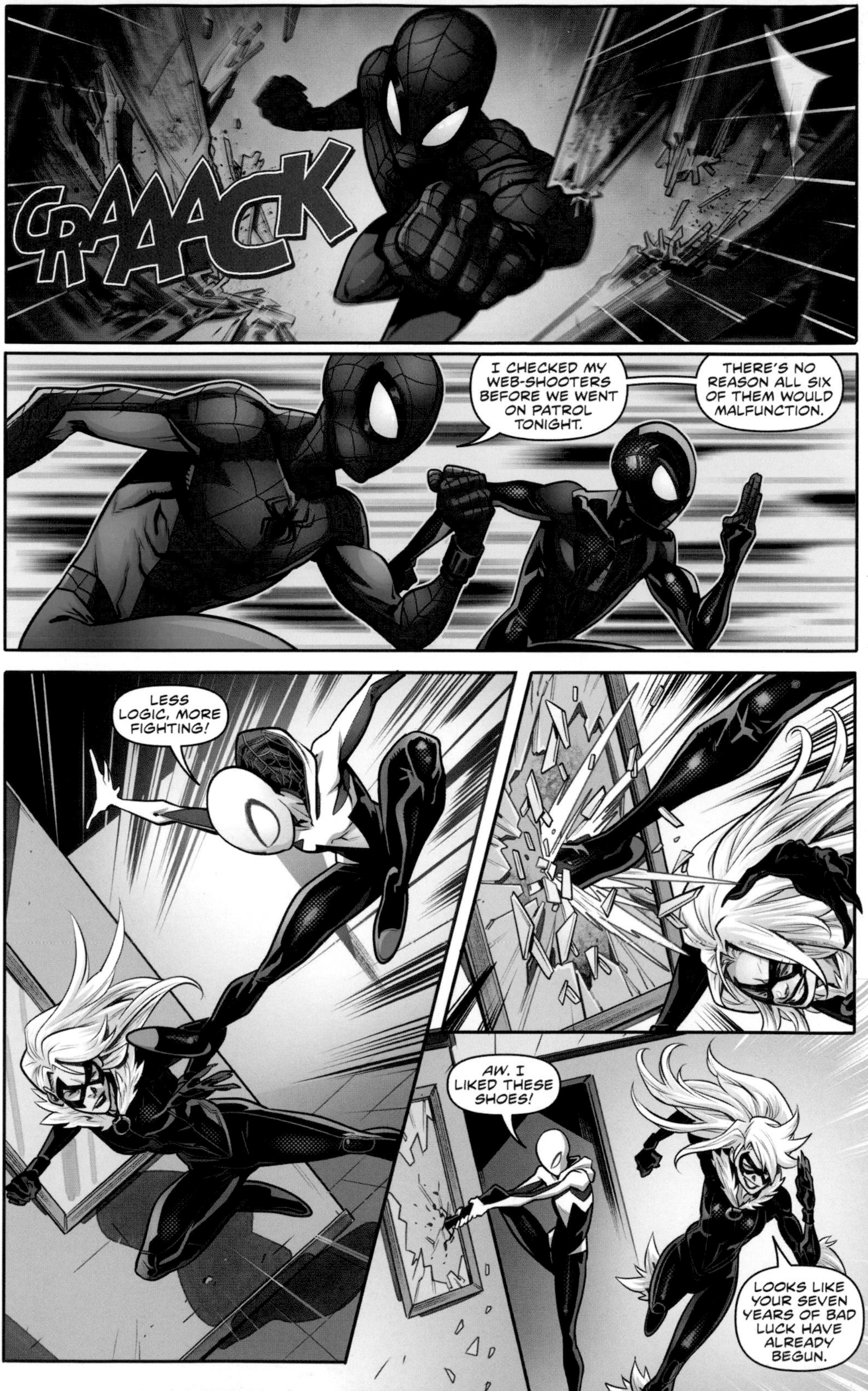

CRAAACK
I CHECKED MY WEB-SHOOTERS BEFORE WE WENT ON PATROL TONIGHT.
THERE'S NO REASON ALL SIX OF THEM WOULD MALFUNCTION.
LESS LOGIC, MORE FIGHTING!
AW. I LIKED THESE SHOES!
LOOKS LIKE YOUR SEVEN YEARS OF BAD LUCK HAVE ALREADY BEGUN.

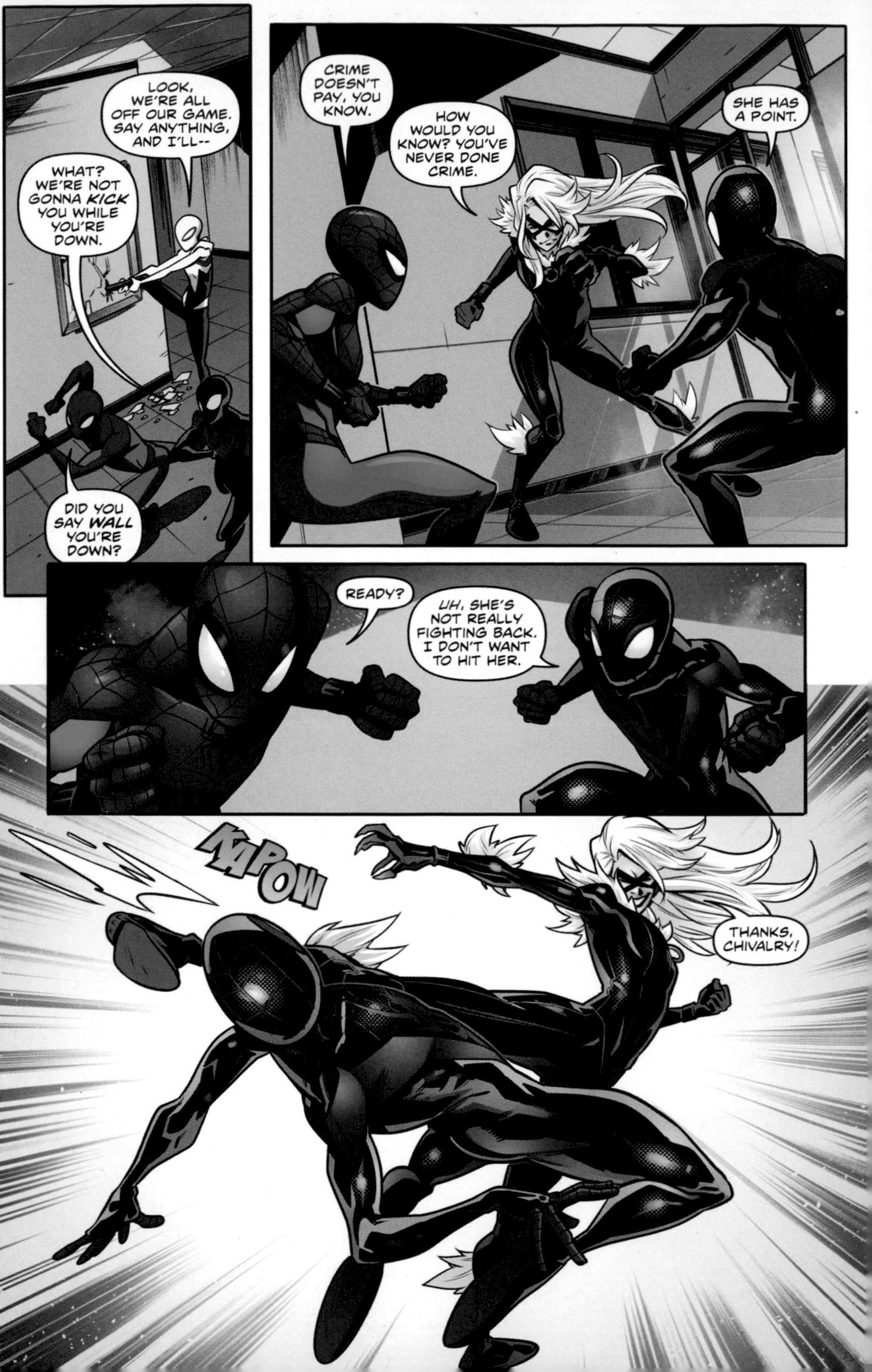
LOOK, WE'RE ALL OFF OUR GAME. SAY ANYTHING, AND I'LL--
WHAT? WE'RE NOT GONNA *KICK* YOU WHILE YOU'RE DOWN.
DID YOU SAY *WALL* YOU'RE DOWN?
CRIME DOESN'T PAY, YOU KNOW.
HOW WOULD YOU KNOW? YOU'VE NEVER DONE CRIME.
SHE HAS A POINT.
READY?
UH, SHE'S NOT REALLY FIGHTING BACK. I DON'T WANT TO HIT HER.
KAPOW
THANKS, CHIVALRY!

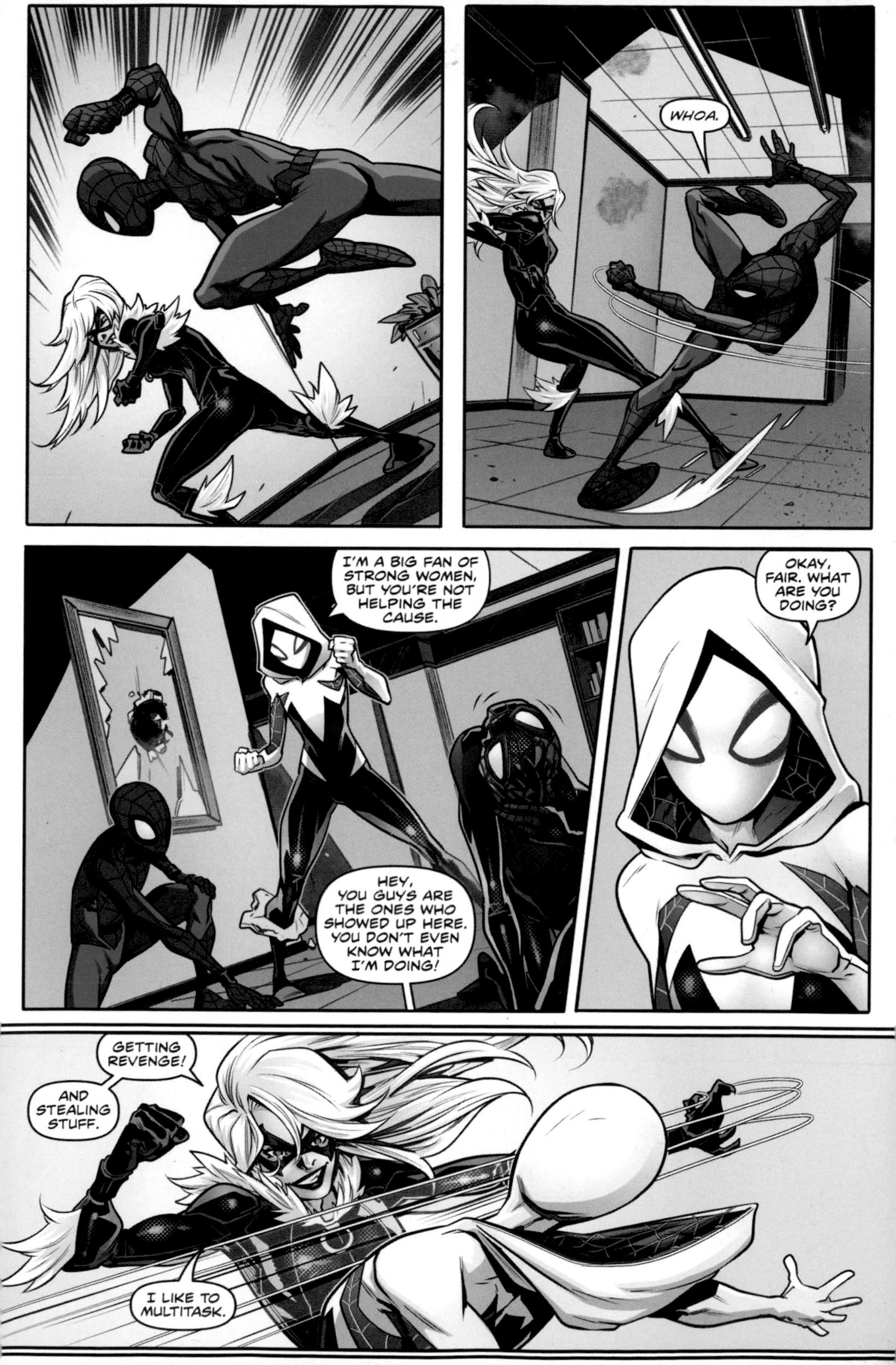
WHOA.
I'M A BIG FAN OF STRONG WOMEN, BUT YOU'RE NOT HELPING THE CAUSE.
HEY, YOU GUYS ARE THE ONES WHO SHOWED UP HERE. YOU DON'T EVEN KNOW WHAT I'M DOING!
OKAY, FAIR. WHAT ARE YOU DOING?
GETTING REVENGE!
AND STEALING STUFF.
I LIKE TO MULTITASK.

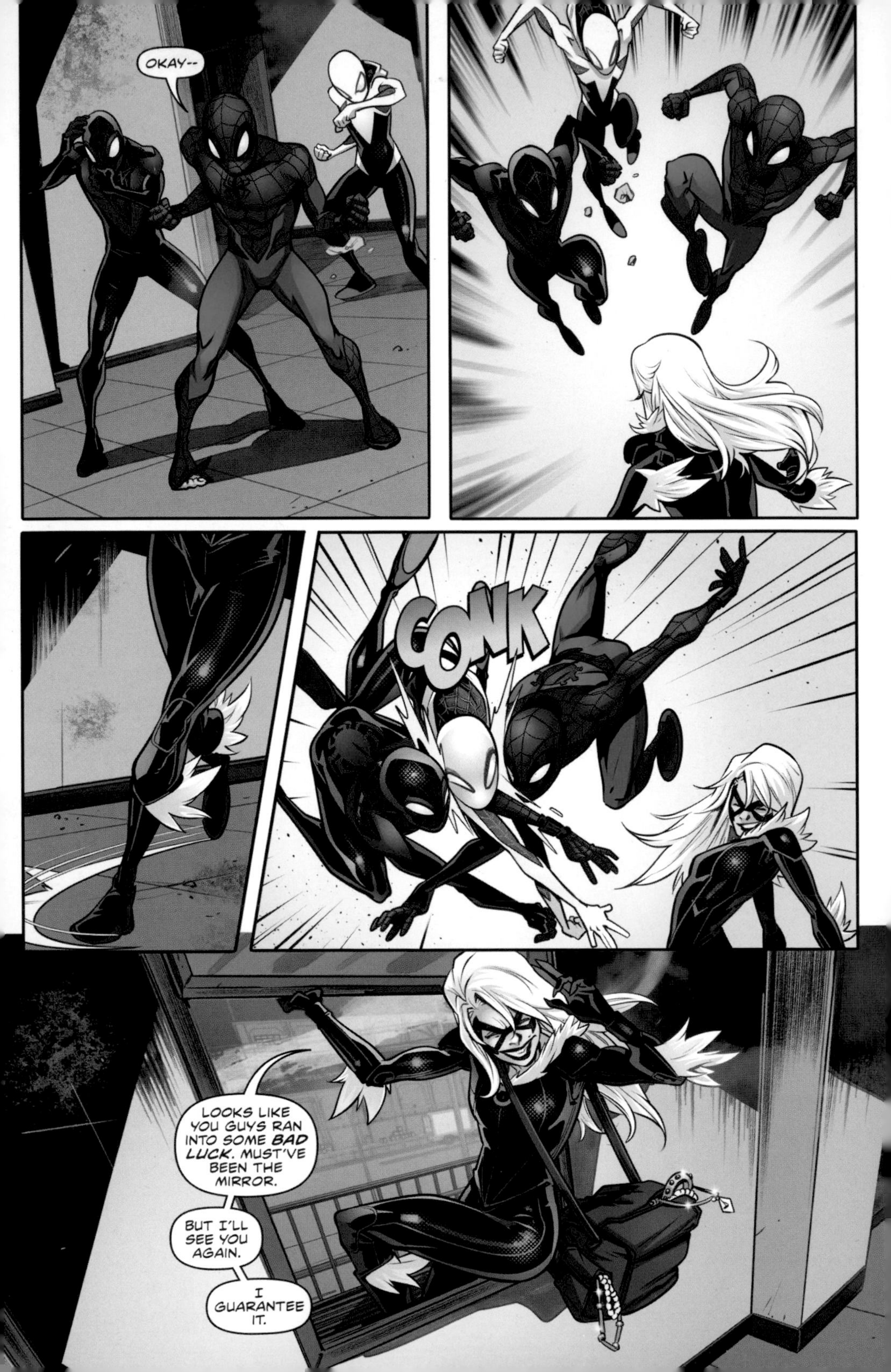
OKAY--
CONK
LOOKS LIKE YOU GUYS RAN INTO SOME BAD LUCK. MUST'VE BEEN THE MIRROR.
BUT I'LL SEE YOU AGAIN.
I GUARANTEE IT.

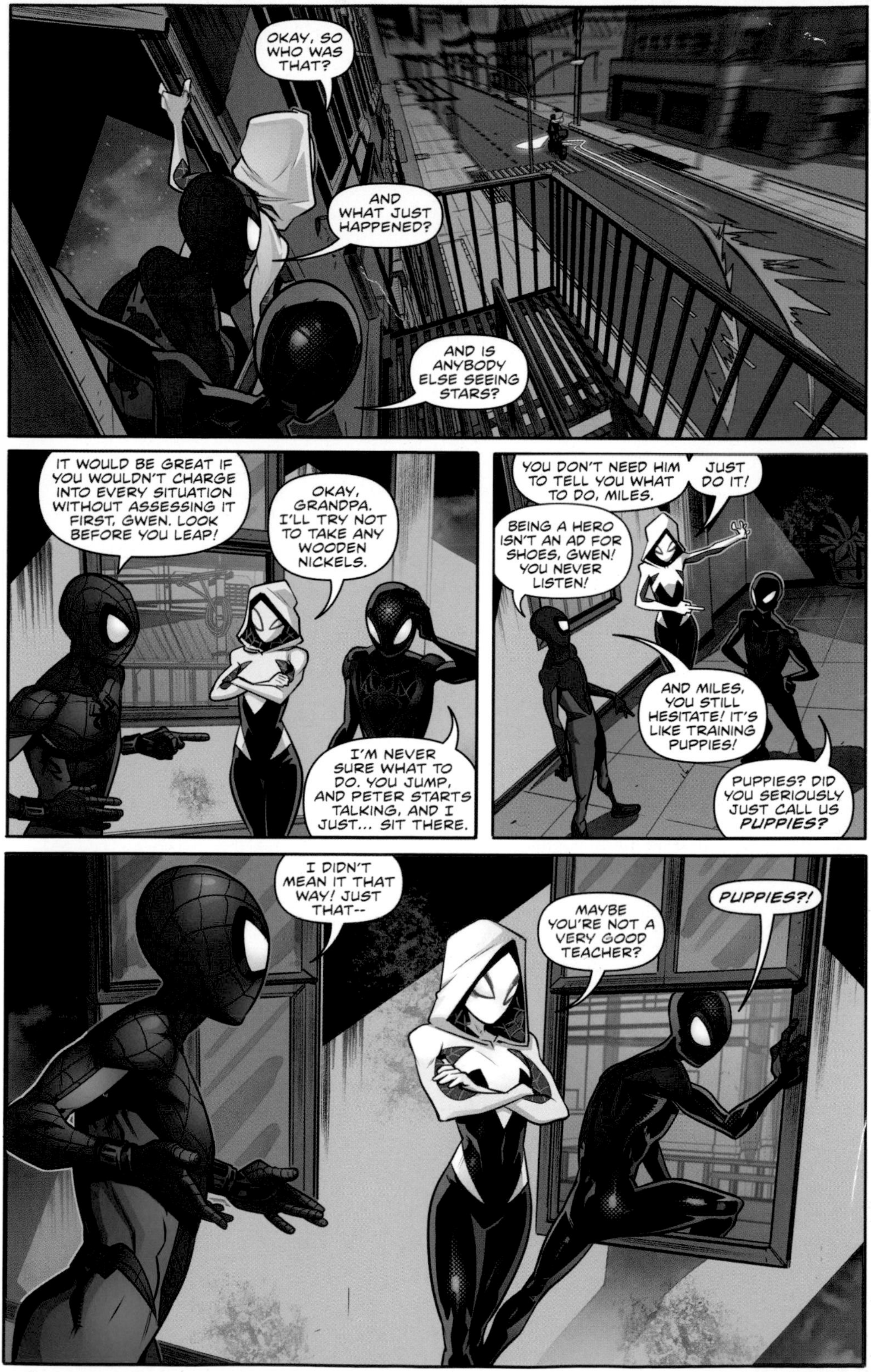
OKAY, SO WHO WAS THAT?
AND WHAT JUST HAPPENED?
AND IS ANYBODY ELSE SEEING STARS?
IT WOULD BE GREAT IF YOU WOULDN'T CHARGE INTO EVERY SITUATION WITHOUT ASSESSING IT FIRST, GWEN. LOOK BEFORE YOU LEAP!
OKAY, GRANDPA. I'LL TRY NOT TO TAKE ANY WOODEN NICKELS.
I'M NEVER SURE WHAT TO DO. YOU JUMP, AND PETER STARTS TALKING, AND I JUST... SIT THERE.
YOU DON'T NEED HIM TO TELL YOU WHAT TO DO, MILES.
JUST DO IT!
BEING A HERO ISN'T AN AD FOR SHOES, GWEN! YOU NEVER LISTEN!
AND MILES, YOU STILL HESITATE! IT'S LIKE TRAINING PUPPIES!
PUPPIES? DID YOU SERIOUSLY JUST CALL US *PUPPIES?*
I DIDN'T MEAN IT THAT WAY! JUST THAT--
MAYBE YOU'RE NOT A VERY GOOD TEACHER?
PUPPIES?!

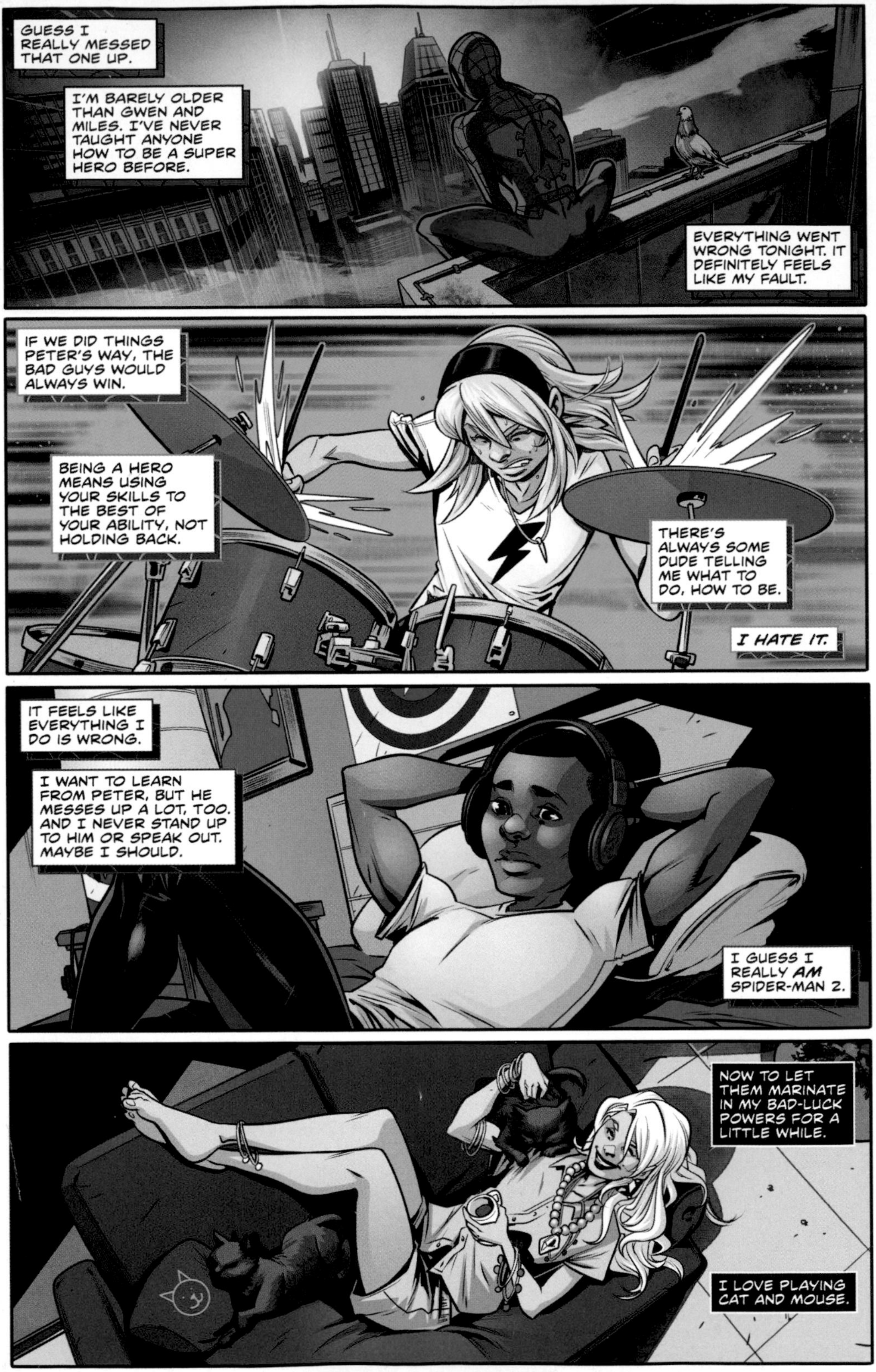
GUESS I REALLY MESSED THAT ONE UP.
I'M BARELY OLDER THAN GWEN AND MILES. I'VE NEVER TAUGHT ANYONE HOW TO BE A SUPER HERO BEFORE.
EVERYTHING WENT WRONG TONIGHT. IT DEFINITELY FEELS LIKE MY FAULT.
IF WE DID THINGS PETER'S WAY, THE BAD GUYS WOULD ALWAYS WIN.
BEING A HERO MEANS USING YOUR SKILLS TO THE BEST OF YOUR ABILITY, NOT HOLDING BACK.
THERE'S ALWAYS SOME DUDE TELLING ME WHAT TO DO, HOW TO BE.
I HATE IT.
IT FEELS LIKE EVERYTHING I DO IS WRONG.
I WANT TO LEARN FROM PETER, BUT HE MESSES UP A LOT, TOO. AND I NEVER STAND UP TO HIM OR SPEAK OUT. MAYBE I SHOULD.
I GUESS I REALLY AM SPIDER-MAN 2.
NOW TO LET THEM MARINATE IN MY BAD-LUCK POWERS FOR A LITTLE WHILE.
I LOVE PLAYING CAT AND MOUSE.

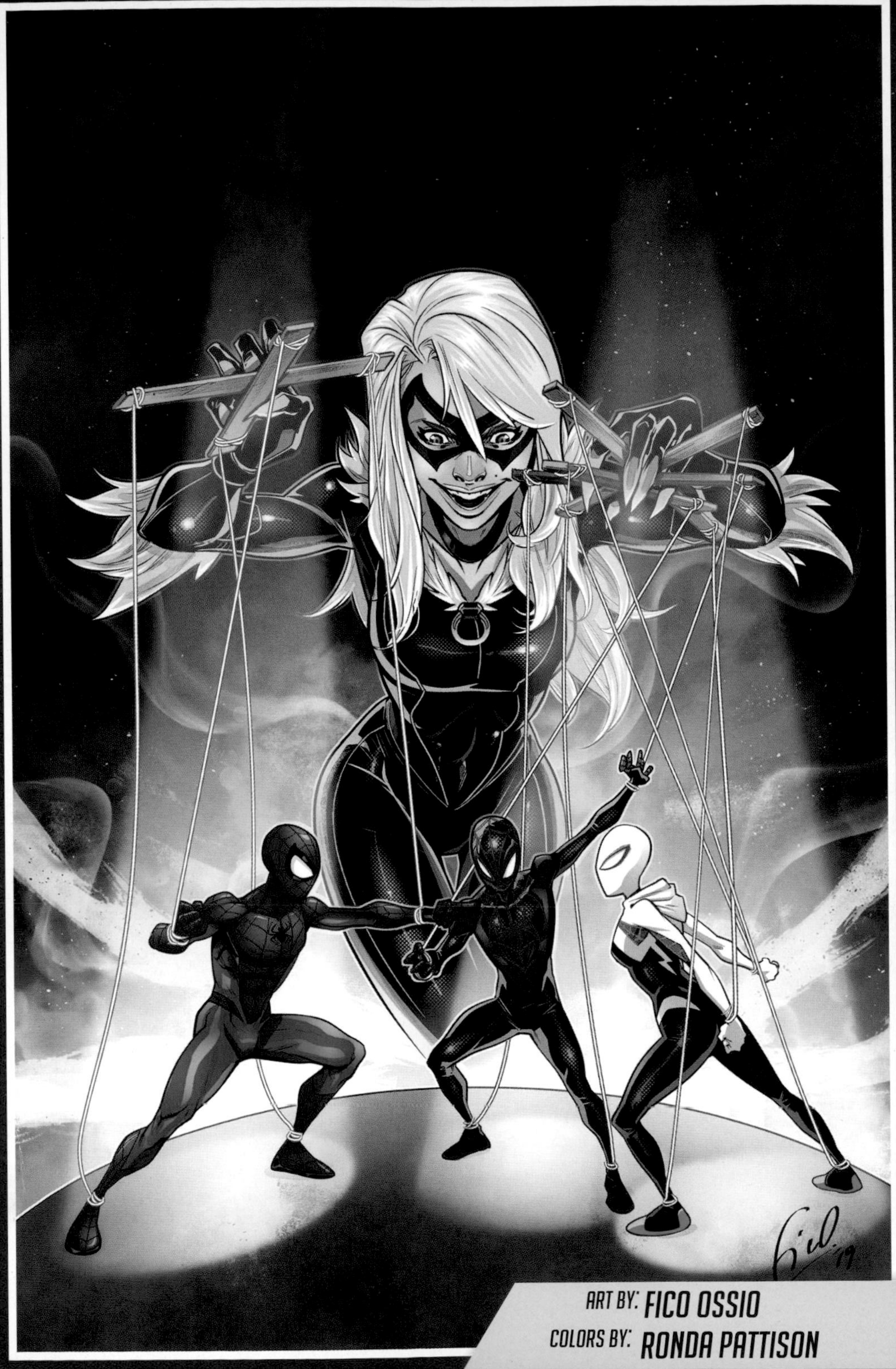
ART BY: FICO OSSIO
COLORS BY: RONDA PATTISON

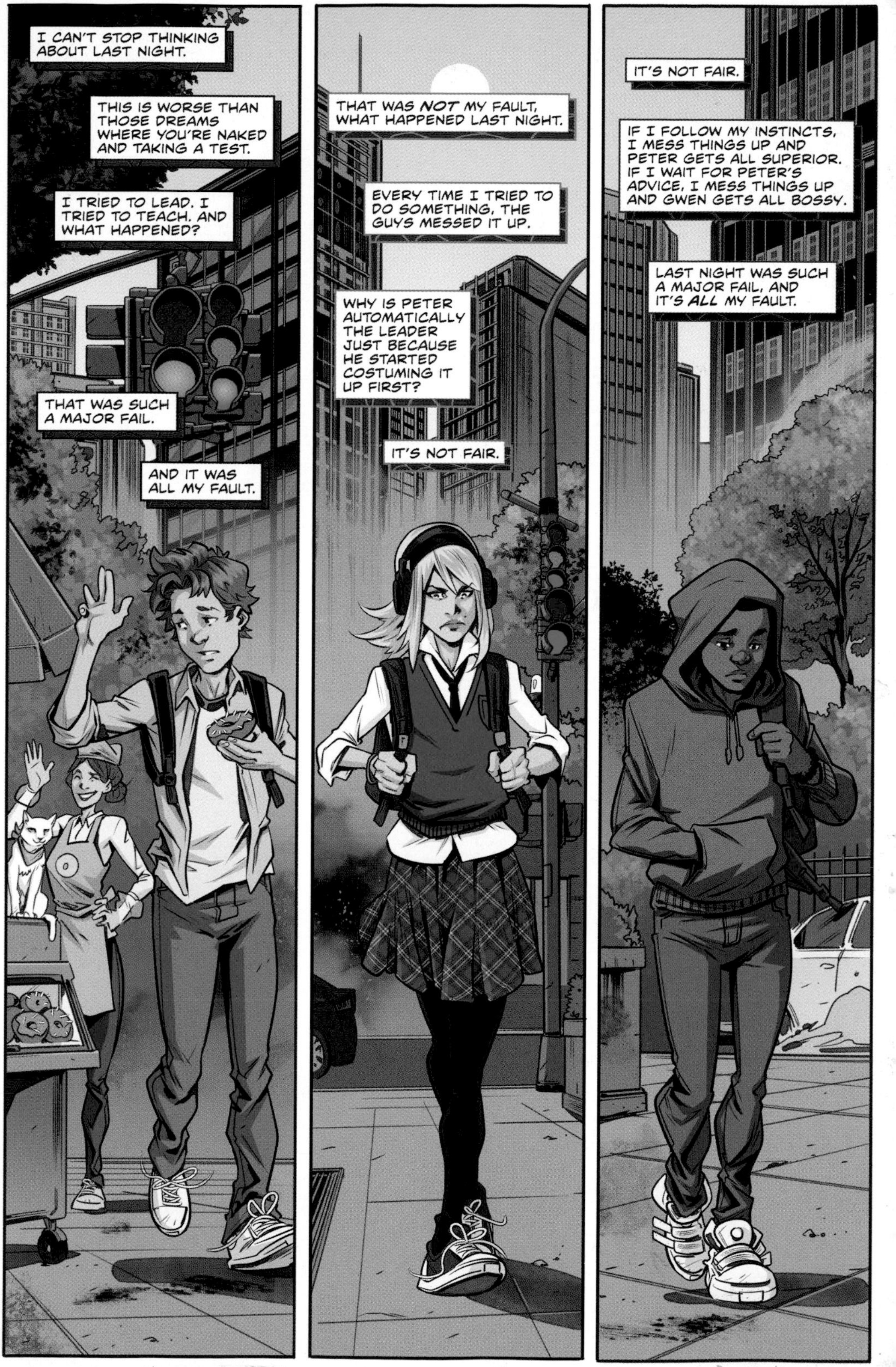
I CAN'T STOP THINKING ABOUT LAST NIGHT.
THIS IS WORSE THAN THOSE DREAMS WHERE YOU'RE NAKED AND TAKING A TEST.
I TRIED TO LEAD. I TRIED TO TEACH. AND WHAT HAPPENED?
THAT WAS SUCH A MAJOR FAIL.
AND IT WAS ALL MY FAULT.
THAT WAS *NOT* MY FAULT, WHAT HAPPENED LAST NIGHT.
EVERY TIME I TRIED TO DO SOMETHING, THE GUYS MESSED IT UP.
WHY IS PETER AUTOMATICALLY THE LEADER JUST BECAUSE HE STARTED COSTUMING IT UP FIRST?
IT'S NOT FAIR.
IT'S NOT FAIR.
IF I FOLLOW MY INSTINCTS, I MESS THINGS UP AND PETER GETS ALL SUPERIOR. IF I WAIT FOR PETER'S ADVICE, I MESS THINGS UP AND GWEN GETS ALL BOSSY.
LAST NIGHT WAS SUCH A MAJOR FAIL, AND IT'S *ALL* MY FAULT.

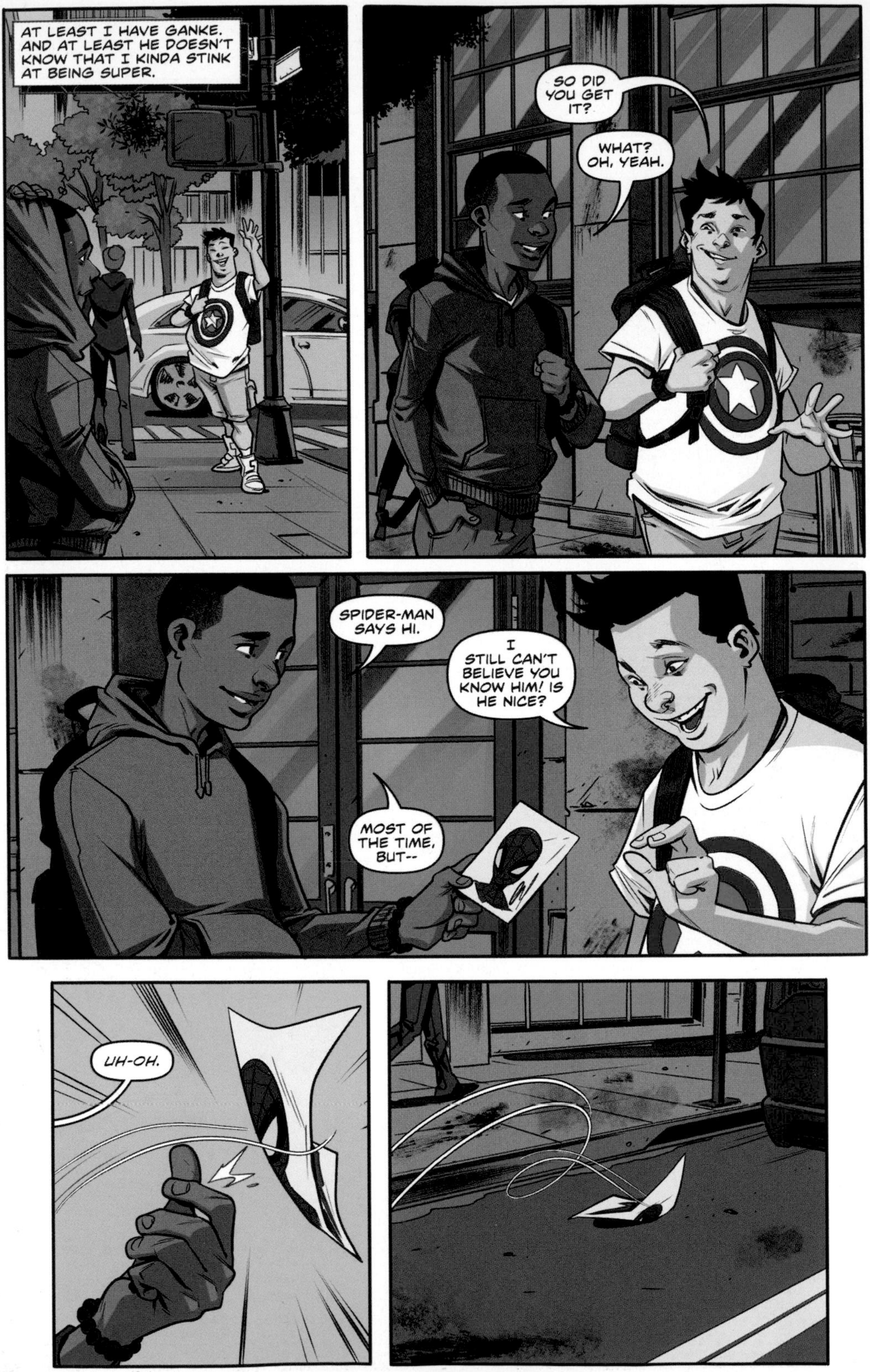
AT LEAST I HAVE GANKE. AND AT LEAST HE DOESN'T KNOW THAT I KINDA STINK AT BEING SUPER.
SO DID YOU GET IT?
WHAT? OH, YEAH.
SPIDER-MAN SAYS HI.
I STILL CAN'T BELIEVE YOU KNOW HIM! IS HE NICE?
MOST OF THE TIME, BUT--
UH-OH.

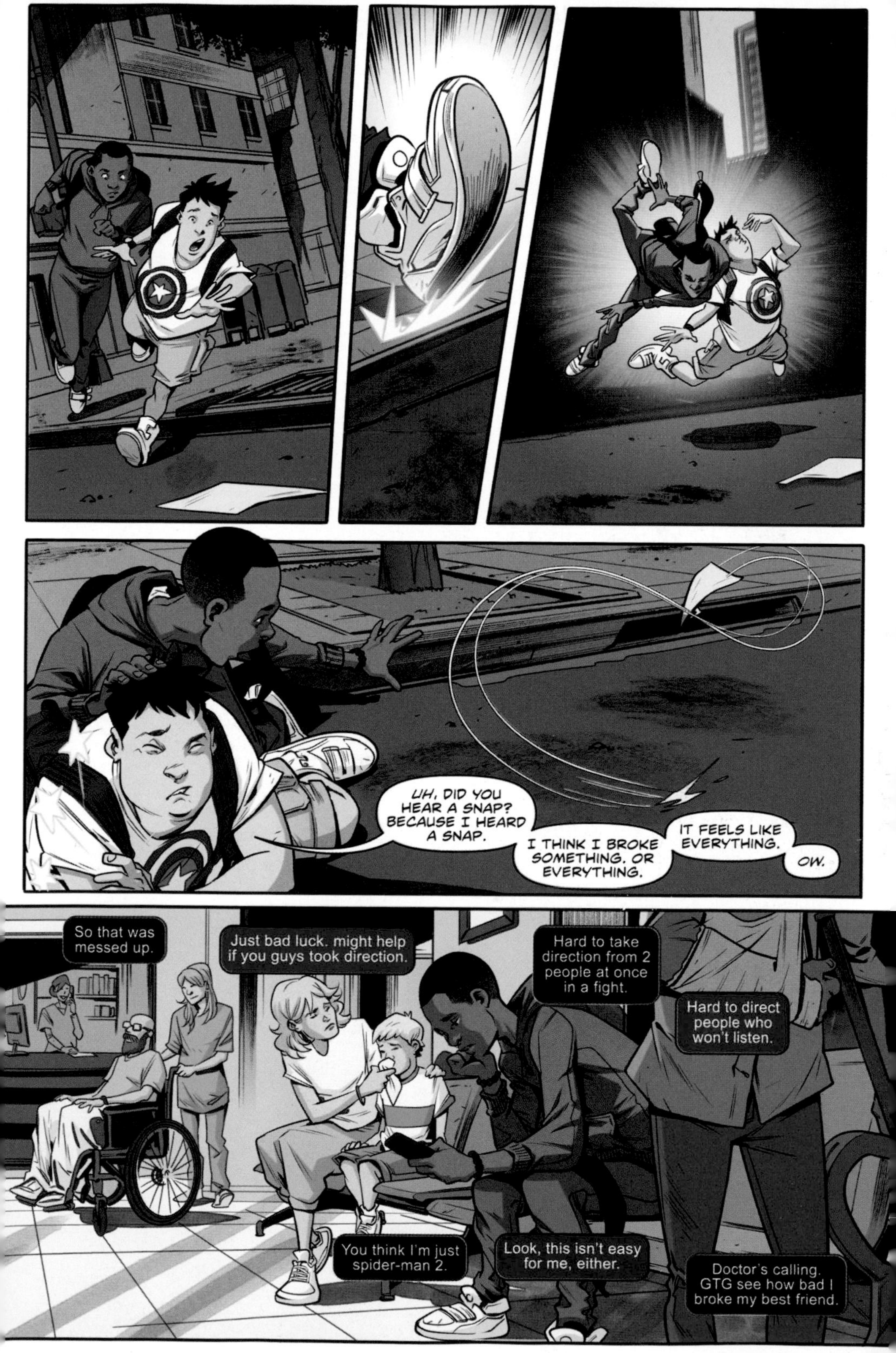
UH, DID YOU HEAR A SNAP? BECAUSE I HEARD A SNAP.
I THINK I BROKE SOMETHING. OR EVERYTHING.
IT FEELS LIKE EVERYTHING.
OW.
So that was messed up.
Just bad luck. might help if you guys took direction.
Hard to take direction from 2 people at once in a fight.
Hard to direct people who won't listen.
You think I'm just spider-man 2.
Look, this isn't easy for me, either.
Doctor's calling. GTG see how bad I broke my best friend.

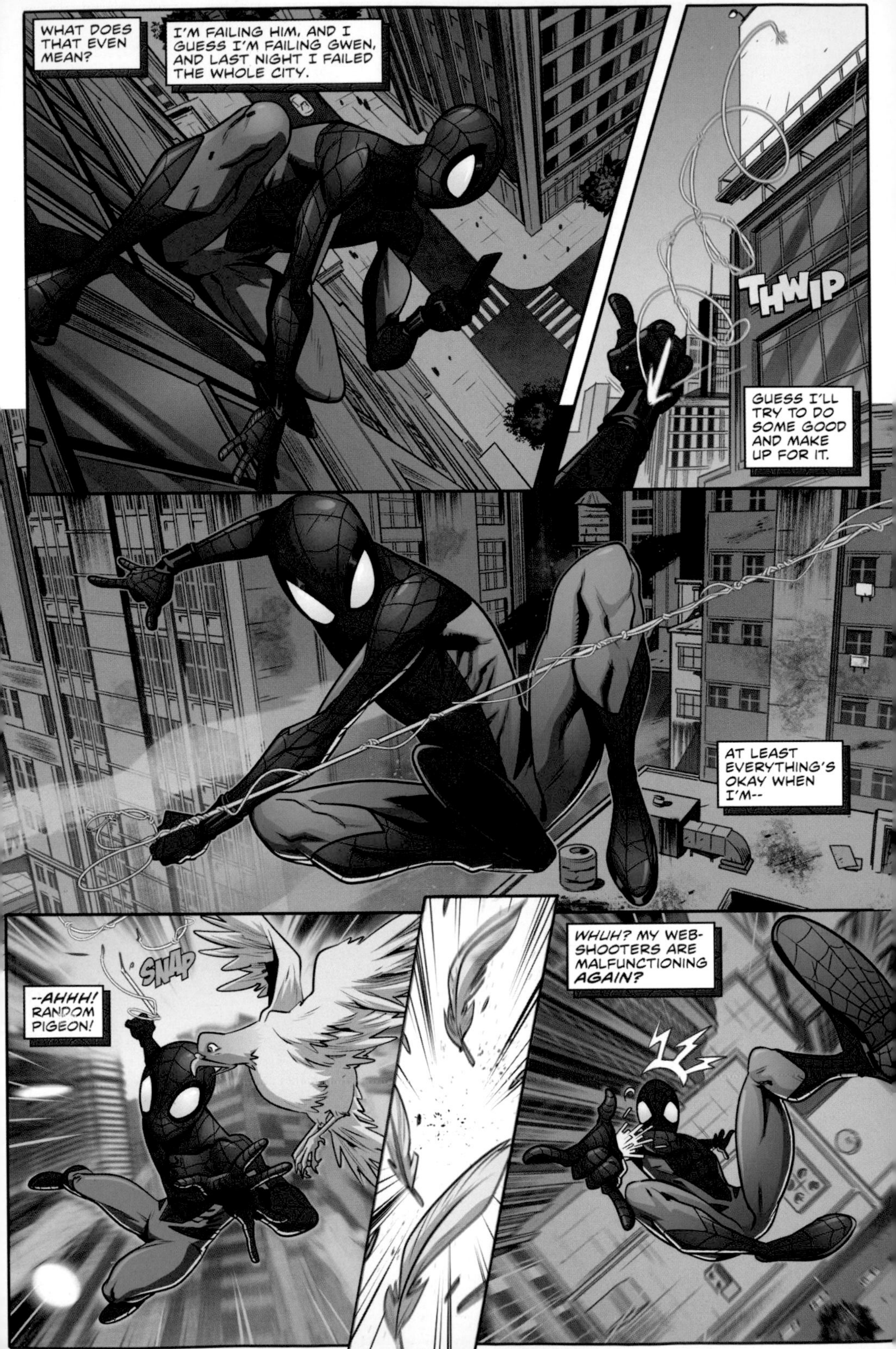
WHAT DOES THAT EVEN MEAN?
I'M FAILING HIM, AND I GUESS I'M FAILING GWEN, AND LAST NIGHT I FAILED THE WHOLE CITY.
THWIP
GUESS I'LL TRY TO DO SOME GOOD AND MAKE UP FOR IT.
AT LEAST EVERYTHING'S OKAY WHEN I'M--
SNAP
--AHHH! RANDOM PIGEON!
WHUH? MY WEB-SHOOTERS ARE MALFUNCTIONING AGAIN?

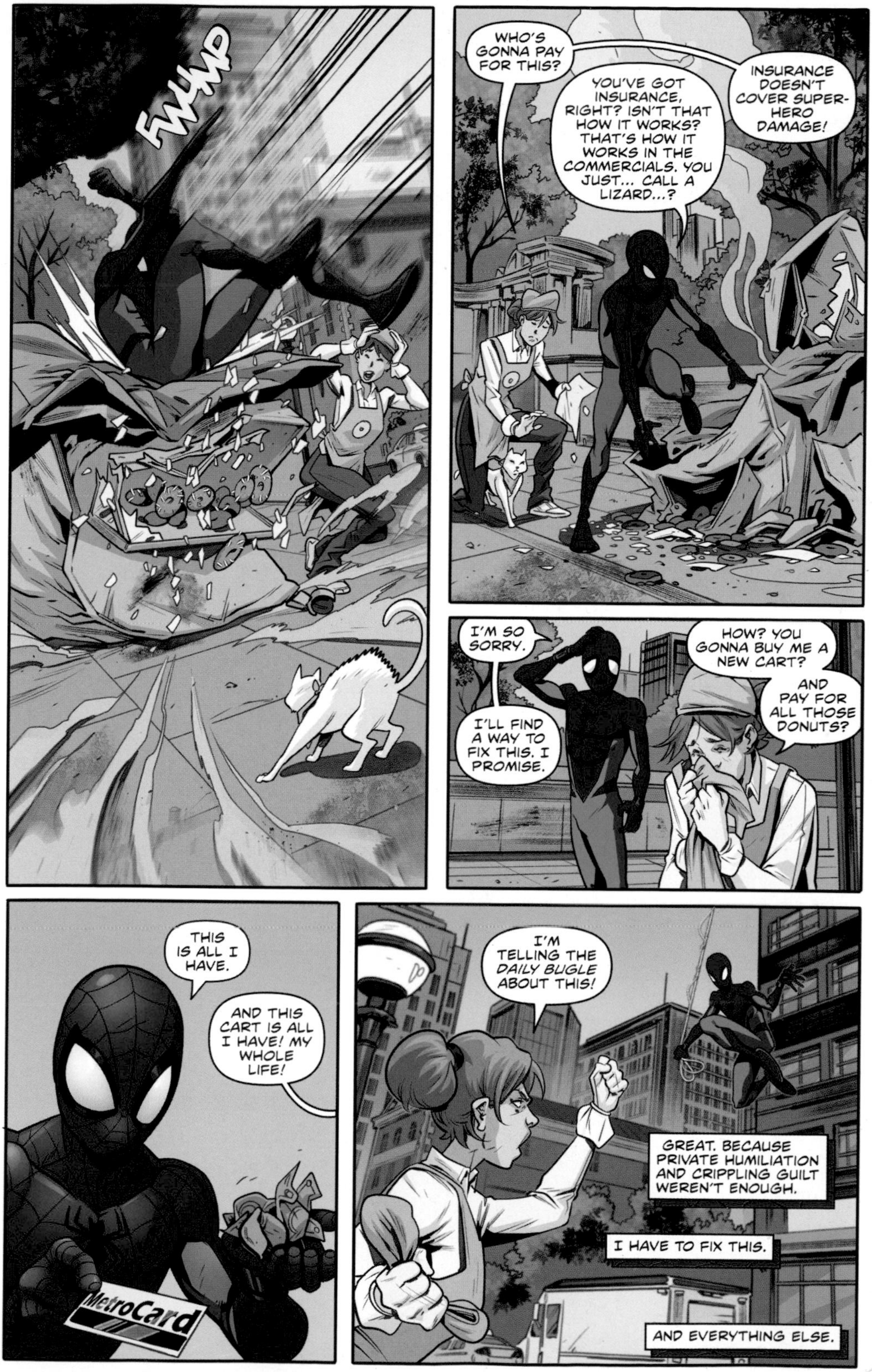
FWUMP
WHO'S GONNA PAY FOR THIS?
YOU'VE GOT INSURANCE, RIGHT? ISN'T THAT HOW IT WORKS? THAT'S HOW IT WORKS IN THE COMMERCIALS. YOU JUST... CALL A LIZARD...?
INSURANCE DOESN'T COVER SUPER-HERO DAMAGE!
I'M SO SORRY.
I'LL FIND A WAY TO FIX THIS. I PROMISE.
HOW? YOU GONNA BUY ME A NEW CART?
AND PAY FOR ALL THOSE DONUTS?
THIS IS ALL I HAVE.
AND THIS CART IS ALL I HAVE! MY WHOLE LIFE!
MetroCard
I'M TELLING THE *DAILY BUGLE* ABOUT THIS!
GREAT. BECAUSE PRIVATE HUMILIATION AND CRIPPLING GUILT WEREN'T ENOUGH.
I HAVE TO FIX THIS.
AND EVERYTHING ELSE.

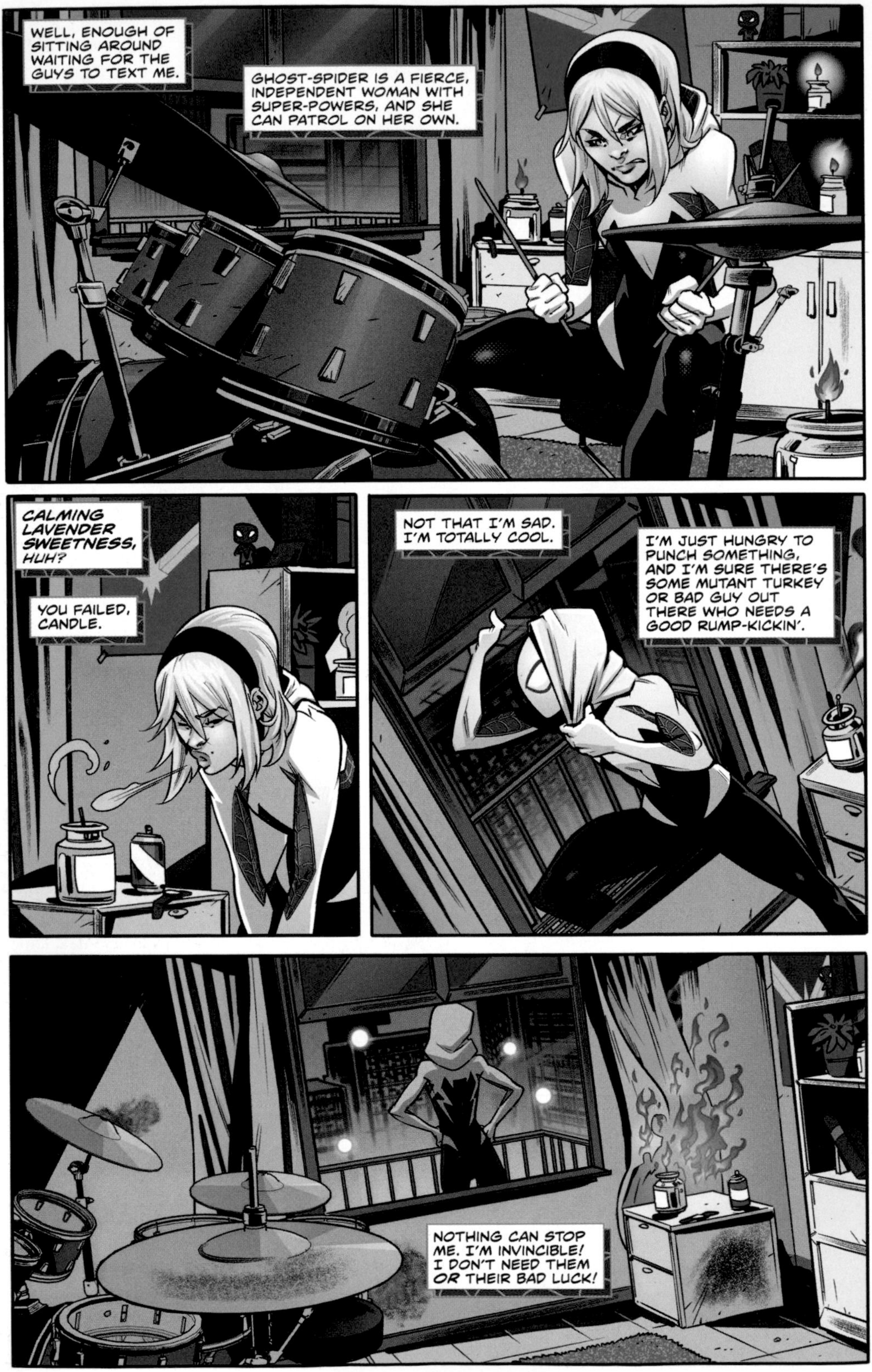
WELL, ENOUGH OF SITTING AROUND WAITING FOR THE GUYS TO TEXT ME.
GHOST-SPIDER IS A FIERCE, INDEPENDENT WOMAN WITH SUPER-POWERS, AND SHE CAN PATROL ON HER OWN.
CALMING LAVENDER SWEETNESS, HUH?
YOU FAILED, CANDLE.
NOT THAT I'M SAD. I'M TOTALLY COOL.
I'M JUST HUNGRY TO PUNCH SOMETHING, AND I'M SURE THERE'S SOME MUTANT TURKEY OR BAD GUY OUT THERE WHO NEEDS A GOOD RUMP-KICKIN'.
NOTHING CAN STOP ME. I'M INVINCIBLE! I DON'T NEED THEM OR THEIR BAD LUCK!

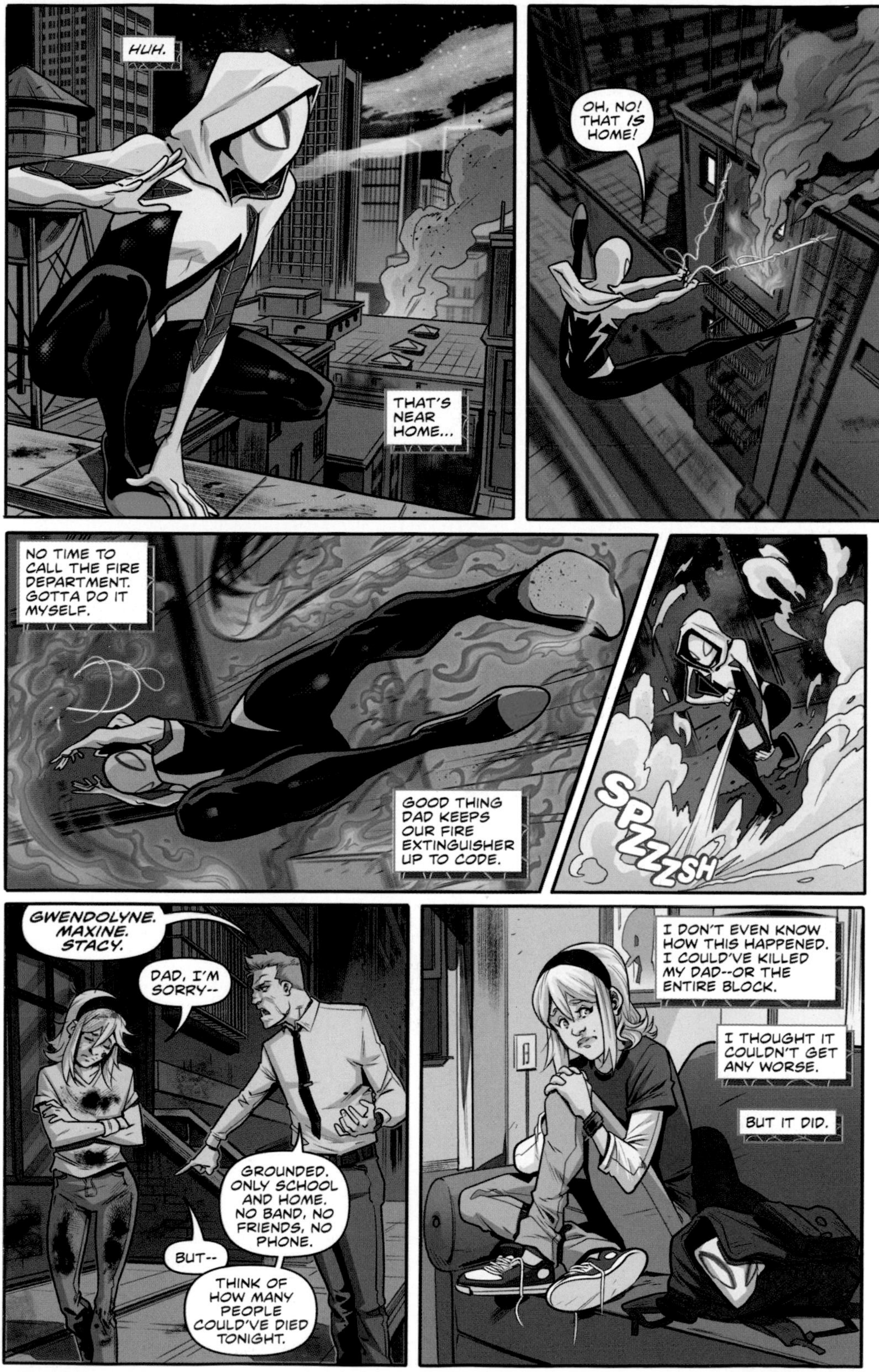
HUH.
THAT'S NEAR HOME...
OH, NO! THAT IS HOME!
NO TIME TO CALL THE FIRE DEPARTMENT. GOTTA DO IT MYSELF.
GOOD THING DAD KEEPS OUR FIRE EXTINGUISHER UP TO CODE.
SPZZZSH
GWENDOLYNE. MAXINE. STACY.
DAD, I'M SORRY--
GROUNDED. ONLY SCHOOL AND HOME. NO BAND, NO FRIENDS, NO PHONE.
BUT--
THINK OF HOW MANY PEOPLE COULD'VE DIED TONIGHT.
I DON'T EVEN KNOW HOW THIS HAPPENED. I COULD'VE KILLED MY DAD--OR THE ENTIRE BLOCK.
I THOUGHT IT COULDN'T GET ANY WORSE.
BUT IT DID.

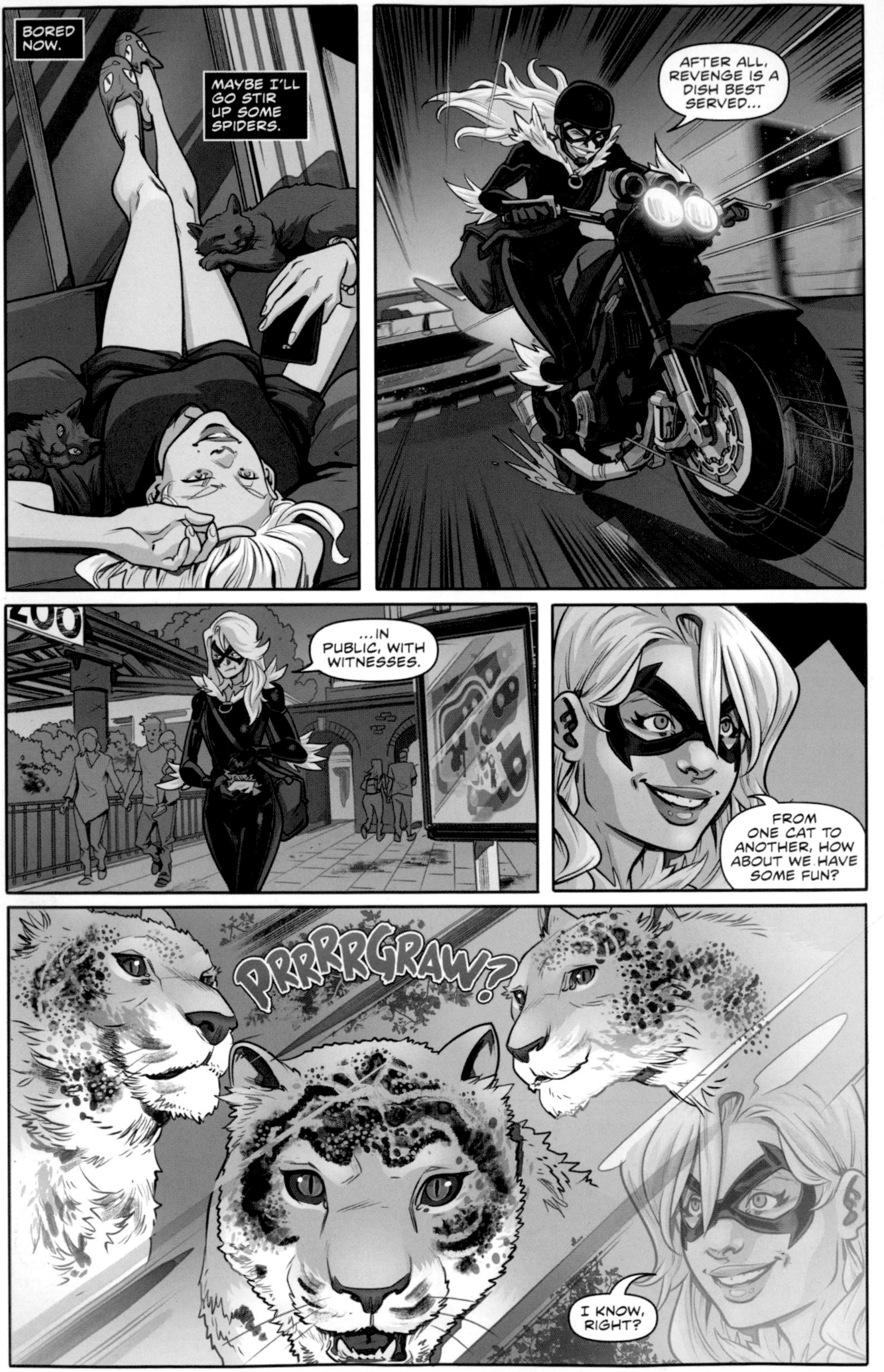
BORED NOW.
MAYBE I'LL GO STIR UP SOME SPIDERS.
AFTER ALL, REVENGE IS A DISH BEST SERVED...
...IN PUBLIC, WITH WITNESSES.
FROM ONE CAT TO ANOTHER, HOW ABOUT WE HAVE SOME FUN?
PRRRRGRAW?
I KNOW, RIGHT?

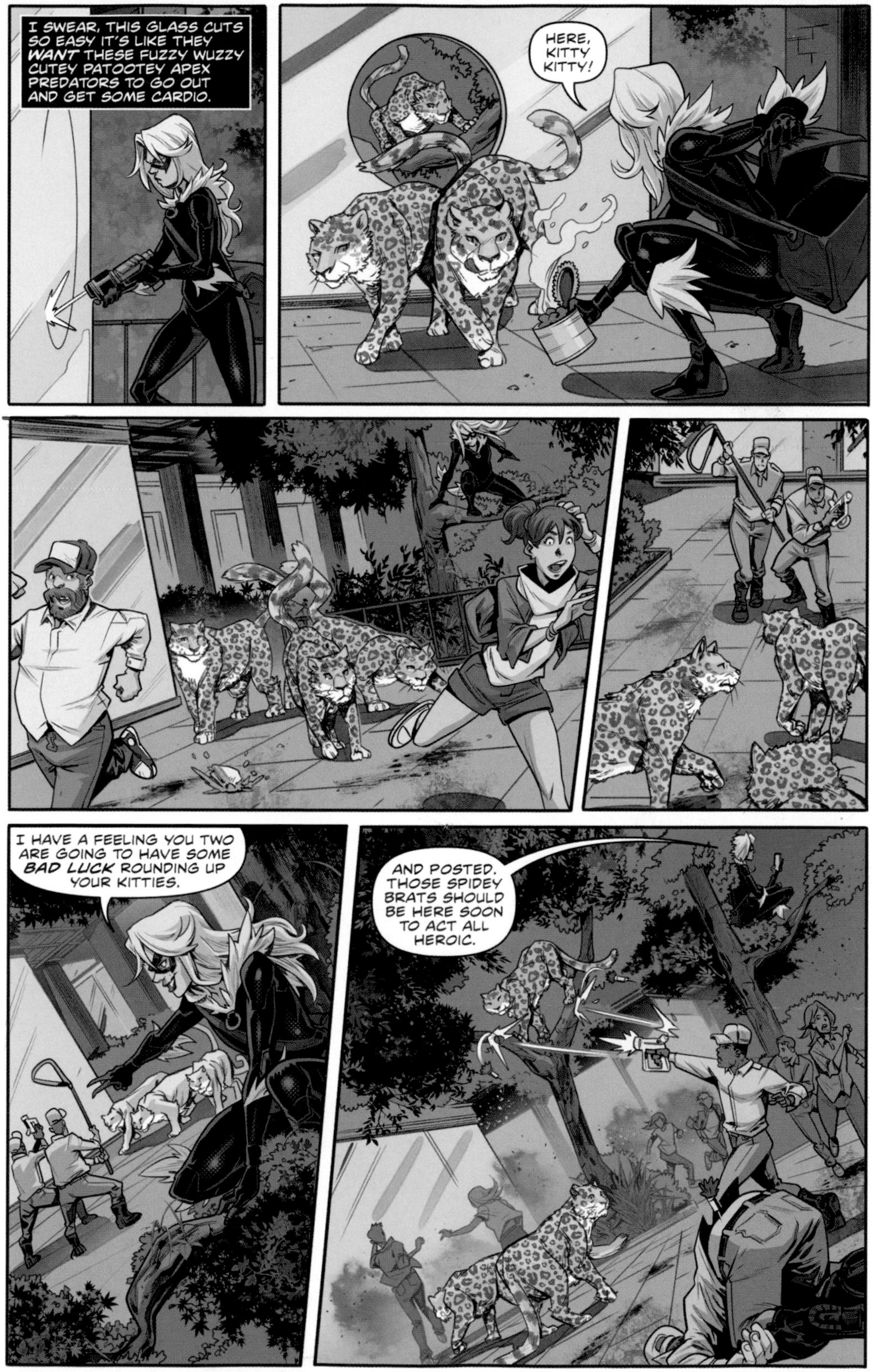
I SWEAR, THIS GLASS CUTS SO EASY IT'S LIKE THEY *WANT* THESE FUZZY WUZZY CUTEY PATOOTEY APEX PREDATORS TO GO OUT AND GET SOME CARDIO.
HERE, KITTY KITTY!
I HAVE A FEELING YOU TWO ARE GOING TO HAVE SOME *BAD LUCK* ROUNDING UP YOUR KITTIES.
AND POSTED. THOSE SPIDEY BRATS SHOULD BE HERE SOON TO ACT ALL HEROIC.

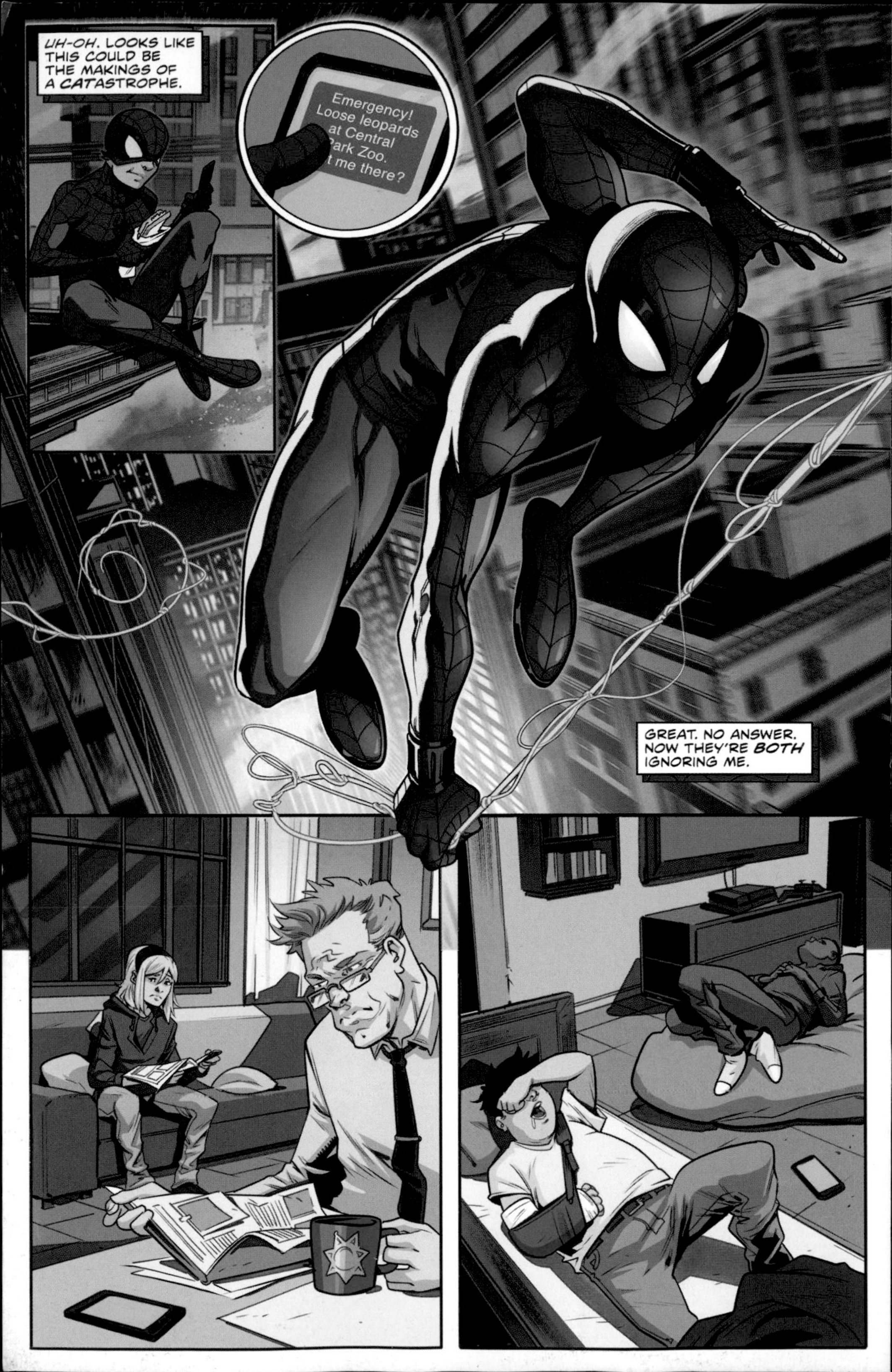
UH-OH. LOOKS LIKE THIS COULD BE THE MAKINGS OF A CATASTROPHE.
Emergency! Loose leopards at Central Park Zoo.
me there?
GREAT. NO ANSWER. NOW THEY'RE BOTH IGNORING ME.

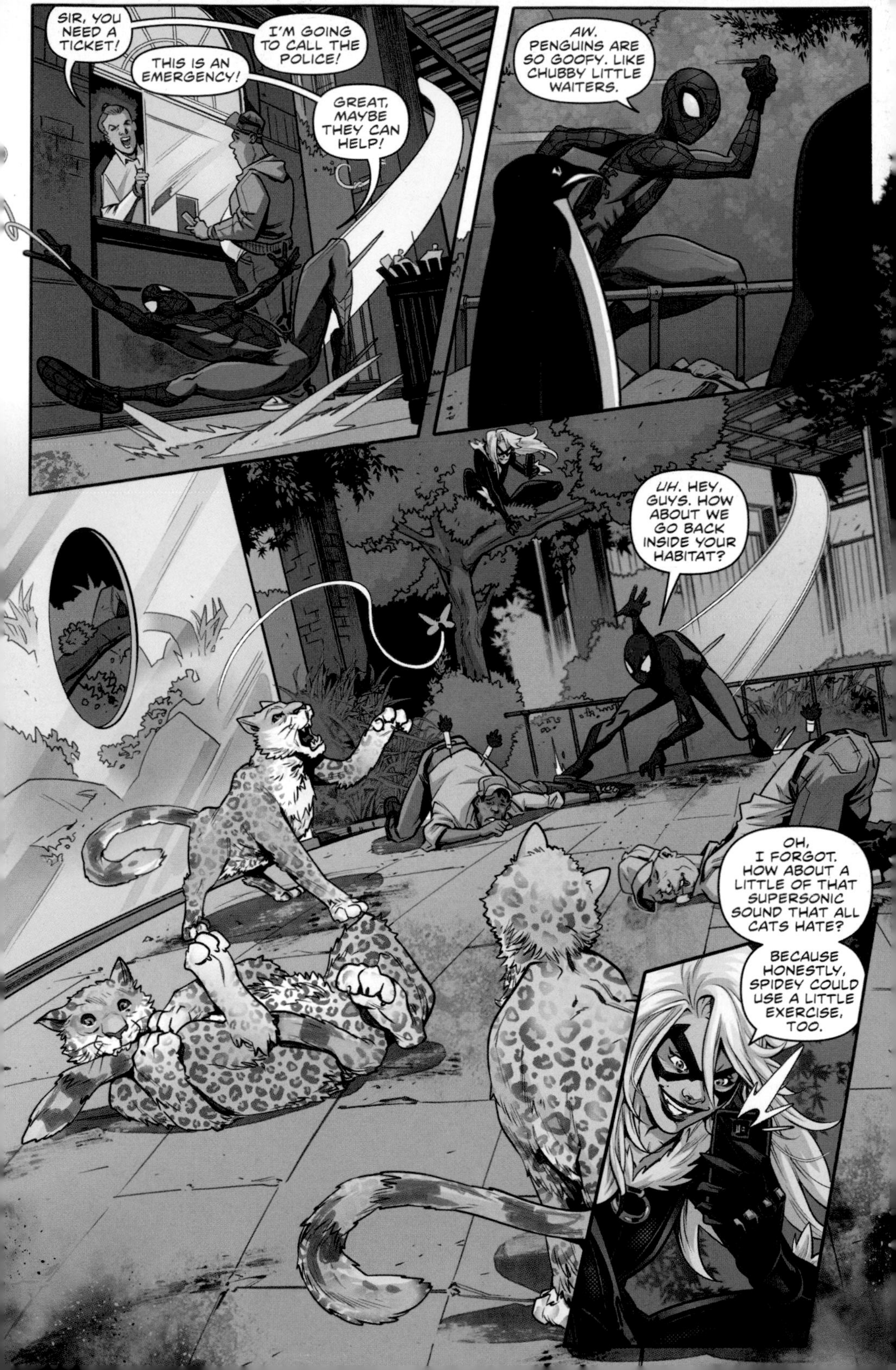
SIR, YOU NEED A TICKET!
I'M GOING TO CALL THE POLICE!
THIS IS AN EMERGENCY!
GREAT, MAYBE THEY CAN HELP!
AW. PENGUINS ARE SO GOOFY. LIKE CHUBBY LITTLE WAITERS.
UH. HEY, GUYS. HOW ABOUT WE GO BACK INSIDE YOUR HABITAT?
OH, I FORGOT. HOW ABOUT A LITTLE OF THAT SUPERSONIC SOUND THAT ALL CATS HATE?
BECAUSE HONESTLY, SPIDEY COULD USE A LITTLE EXERCISE, TOO.

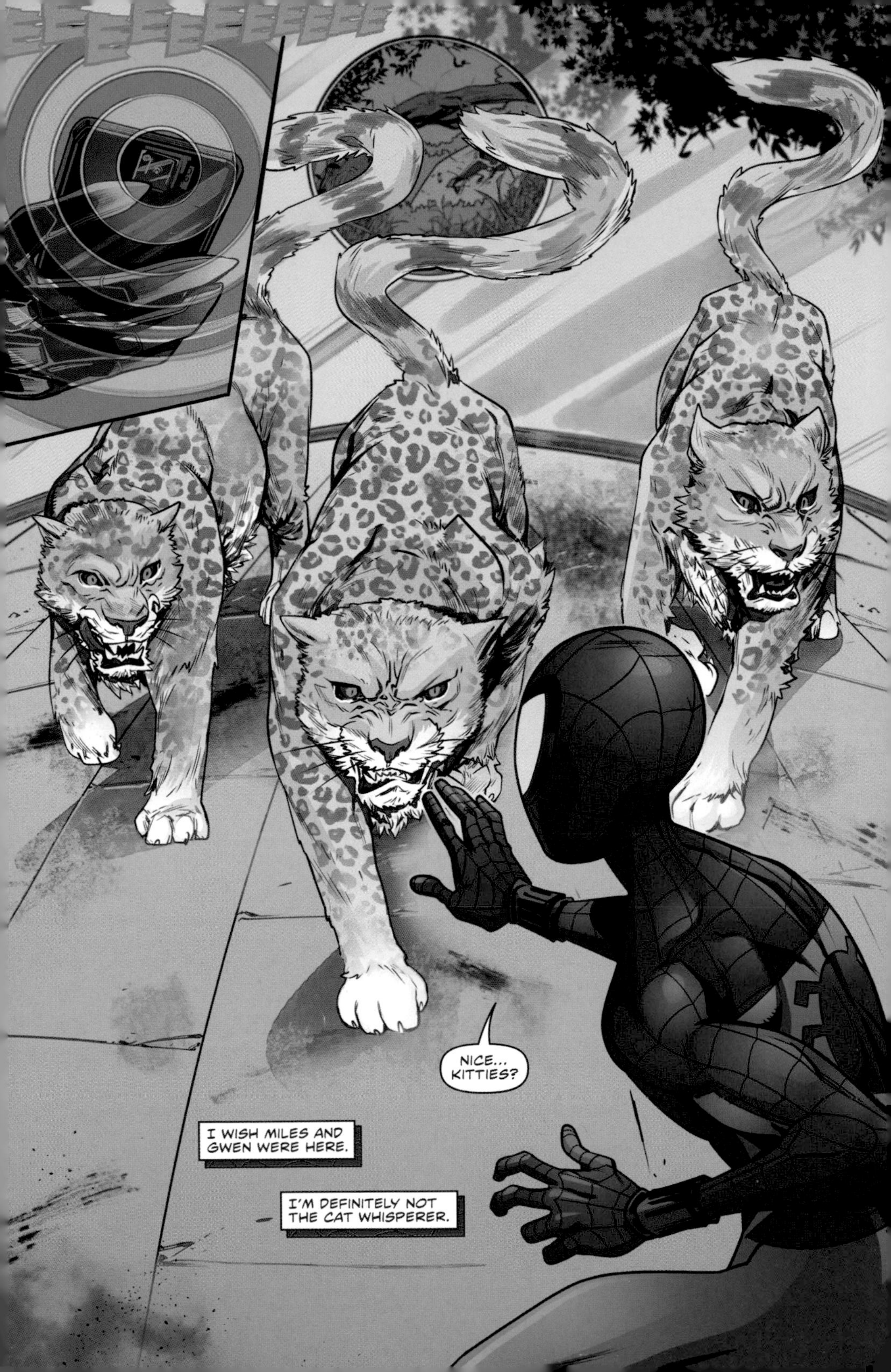
EEEEEEEEEEEEE
NICE... KITTIES?
I WISH MILES AND GWEN WERE HERE.
I'M DEFINITELY NOT THE CAT WHISPERER.

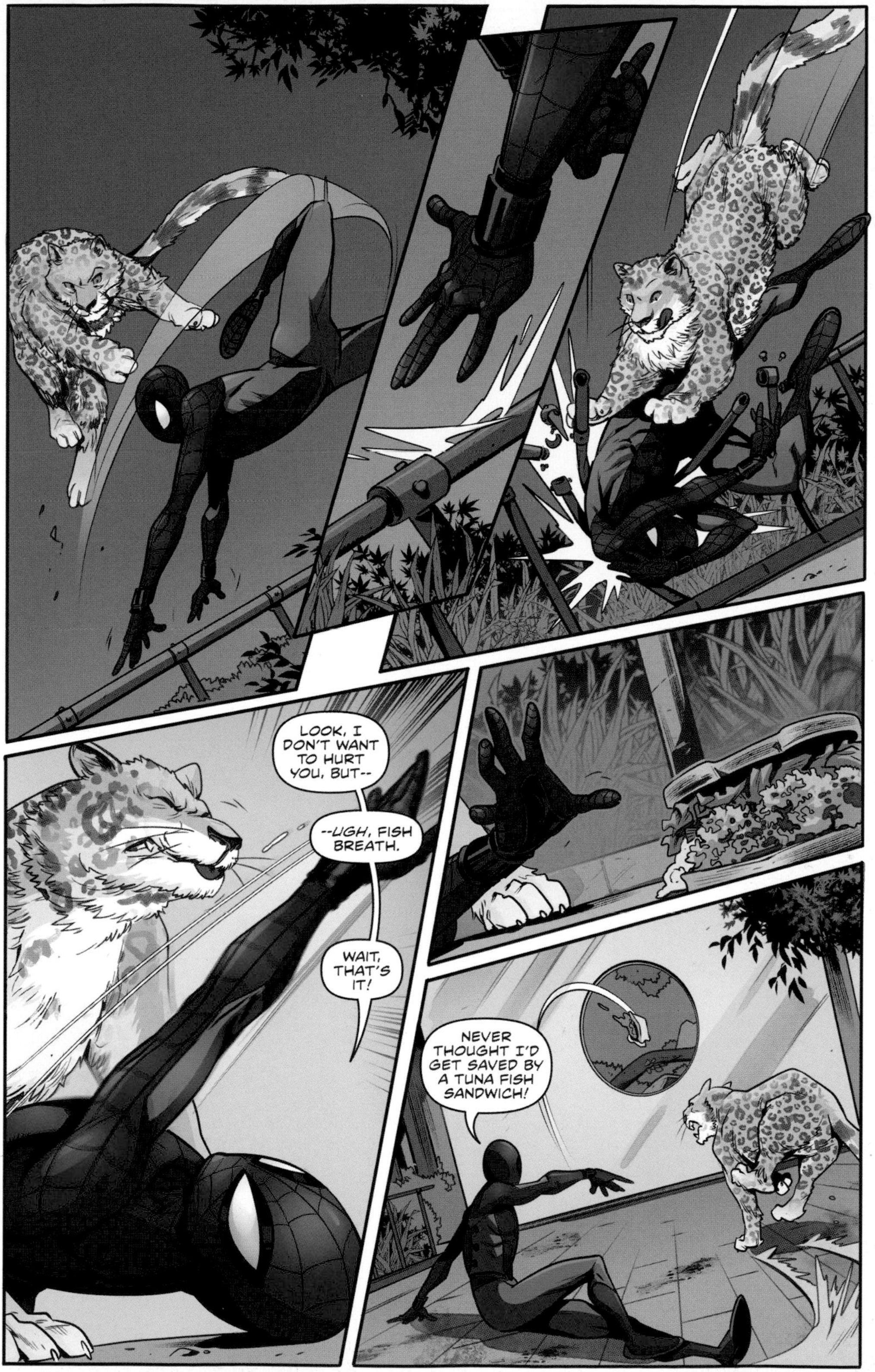
LOOK, I DON'T WANT TO HURT YOU, BUT--
--UGH, FISH BREATH.
WAIT, THAT'S IT!
NEVER THOUGHT I'D GET SAVED BY A TUNA FISH SANDWICH!

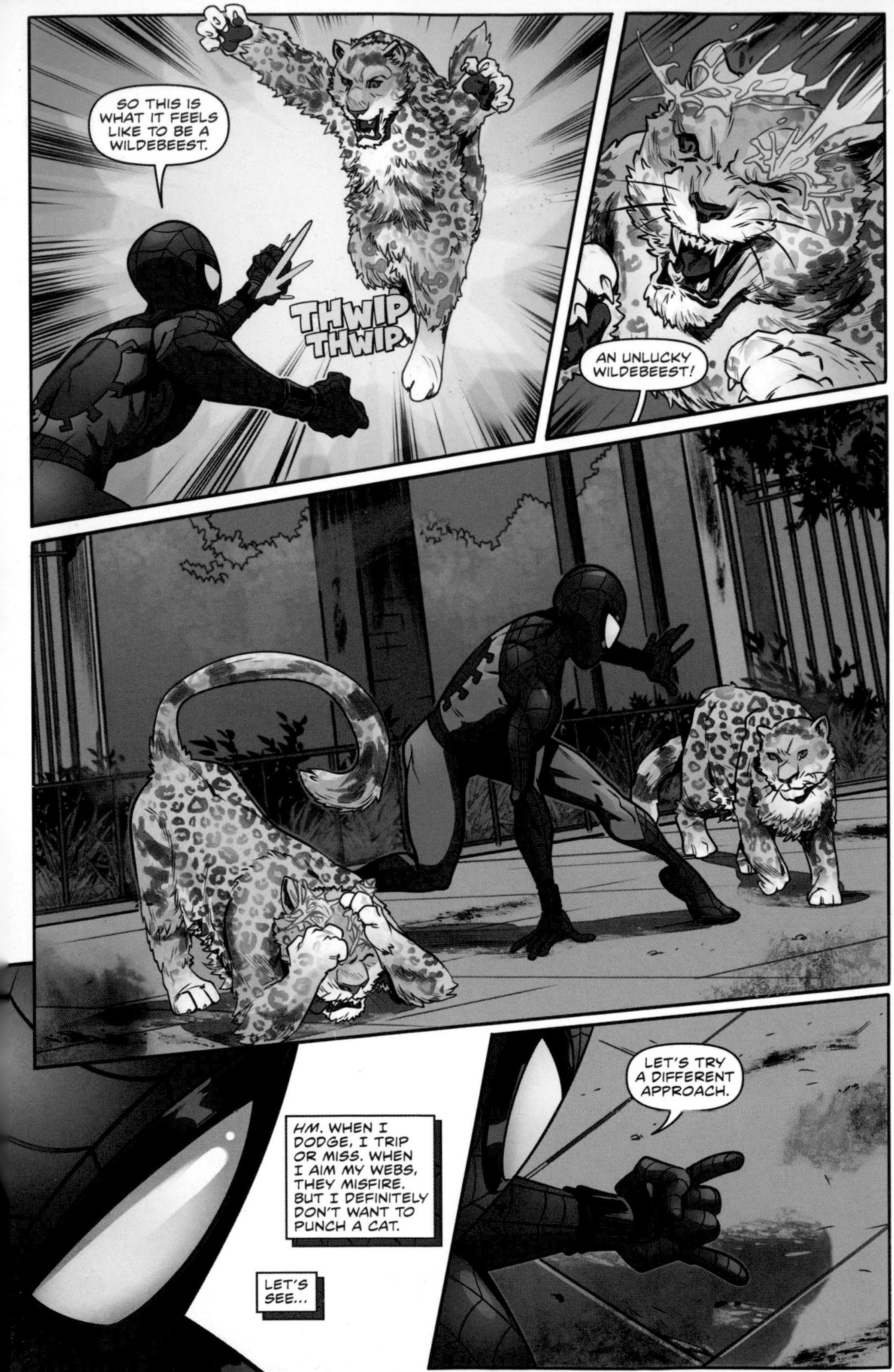
SO THIS IS WHAT IT FEELS LIKE TO BE A WILDEBEEST.
THWIP THWIP
AN UNLUCKY WILDEBEEST!
HM. WHEN I DODGE, I TRIP OR MISS. WHEN I AIM MY WEBS, THEY MISFIRE. BUT I DEFINITELY DON'T WANT TO PUNCH A CAT.
LET'S SEE...
LET'S TRY A DIFFERENT APPROACH.

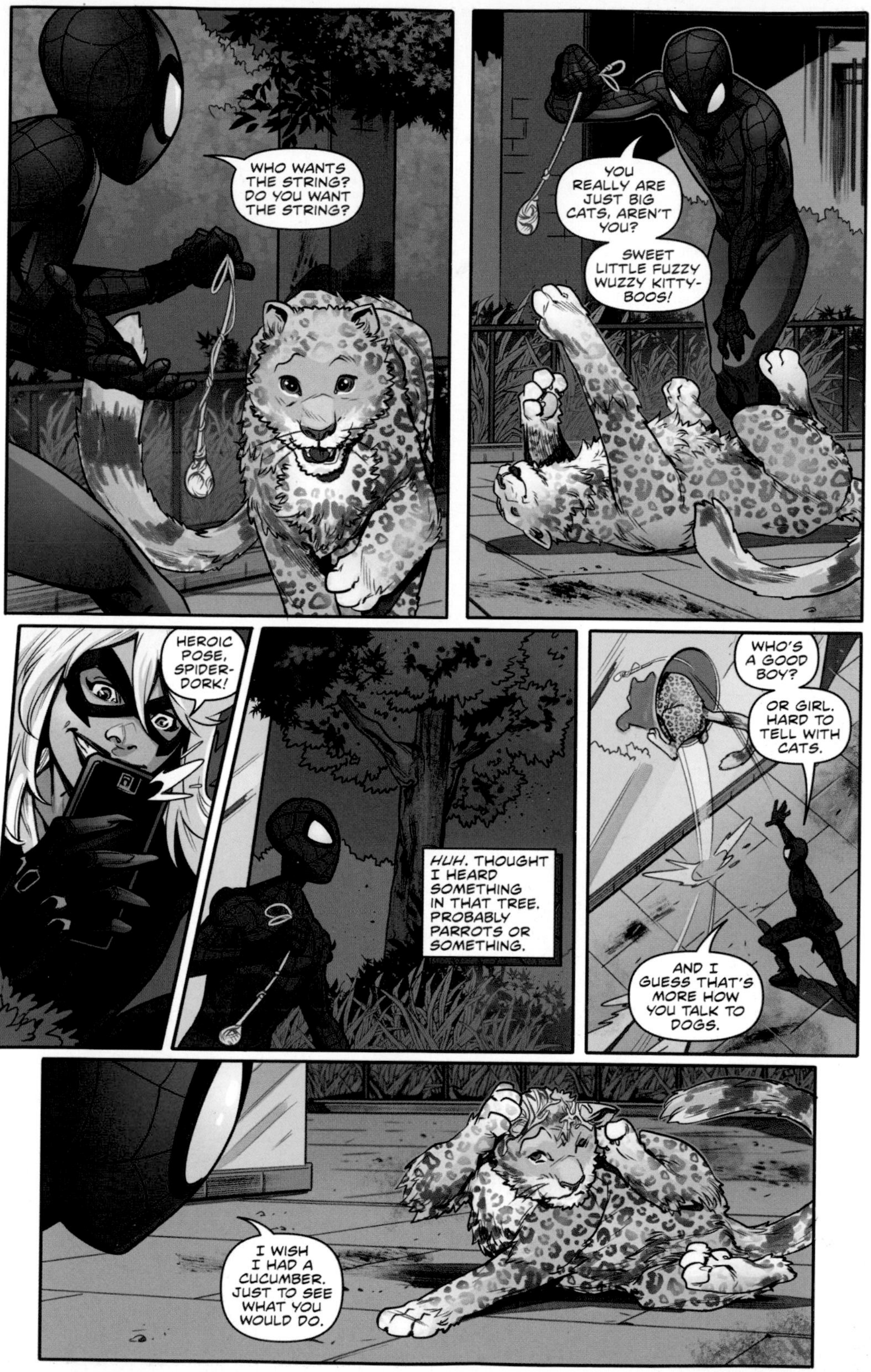
WHO WANTS THE STRING? DO YOU WANT THE STRING?
YOU REALLY ARE JUST BIG CATS, AREN'T YOU?
SWEET LITTLE FUZZY WUZZY KITTY-BOOS!
HEROIC POSE, SPIDER-DORK!
HUH. THOUGHT I HEARD SOMETHING IN THAT TREE. PROBABLY PARROTS OR SOMETHING.
WHO'S A GOOD BOY?
OR GIRL. HARD TO TELL WITH CATS.
AND I GUESS THAT'S MORE HOW YOU TALK TO DOGS.
I WISH I HAD A CUCUMBER. JUST TO SEE WHAT YOU WOULD DO.

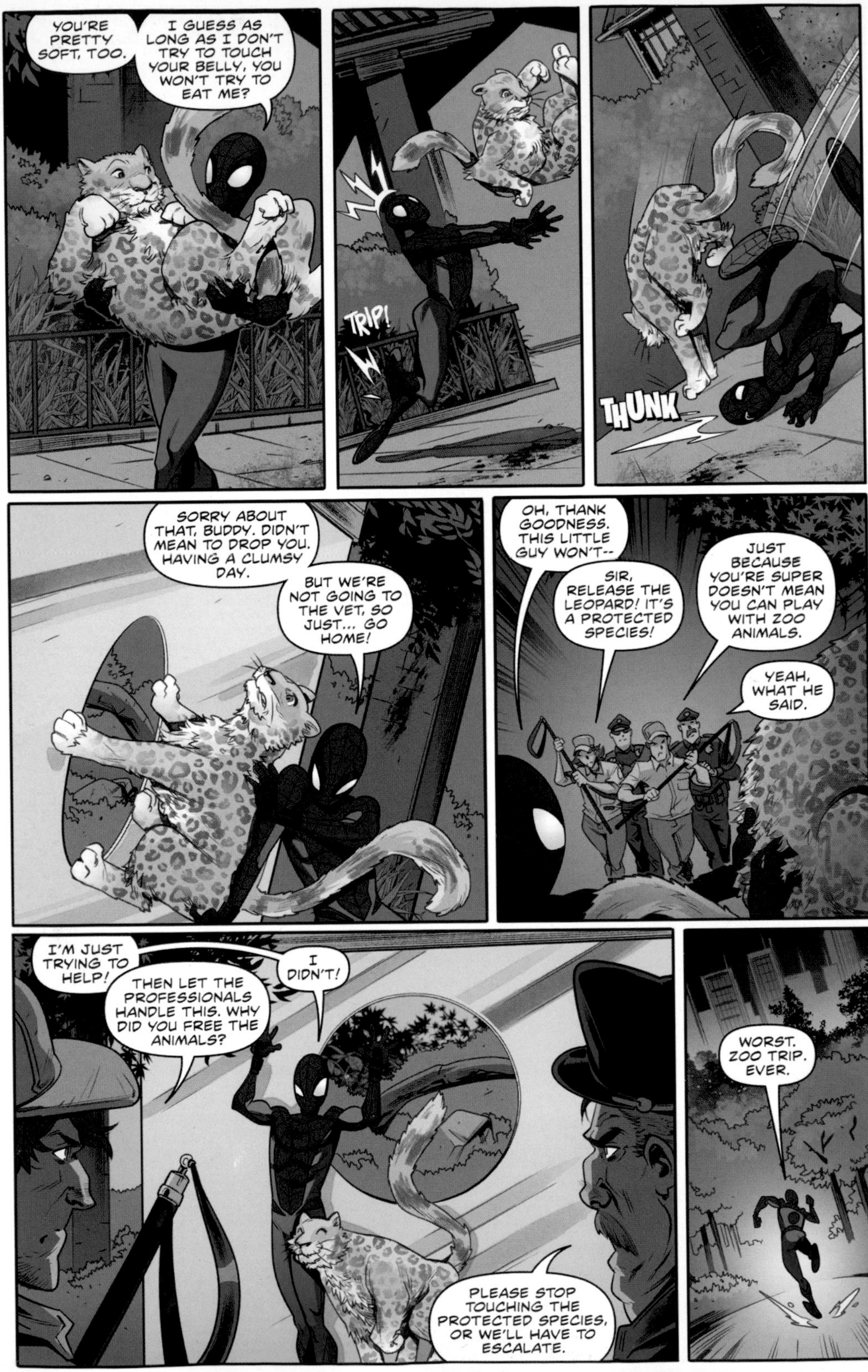

YOU'RE PRETTY SOFT, TOO.
I GUESS AS LONG AS I DON'T TRY TO TOUCH YOUR BELLY, YOU WON'T TRY TO EAT ME?
TRIP!
THUNK
SORRY ABOUT THAT, BUDDY. DIDN'T MEAN TO DROP YOU. HAVING A CLUMSY DAY.
BUT WE'RE NOT GOING TO THE VET, SO JUST... GO HOME!
OH, THANK GOODNESS. THIS LITTLE GUY WON'T--
SIR, RELEASE THE LEOPARD! IT'S A PROTECTED SPECIES!
JUST BECAUSE YOU'RE SUPER DOESN'T MEAN YOU CAN PLAY WITH ZOO ANIMALS.
YEAH, WHAT HE SAID.
I'M JUST TRYING TO HELP!
THEN LET THE PROFESSIONALS HANDLE THIS. WHY DID YOU FREE THE ANIMALS?
I DIDN'T!
PLEASE STOP TOUCHING THE PROTECTED SPECIES, OR WE'LL HAVE TO ESCALATE.
WORST. ZOO TRIP. EVER.

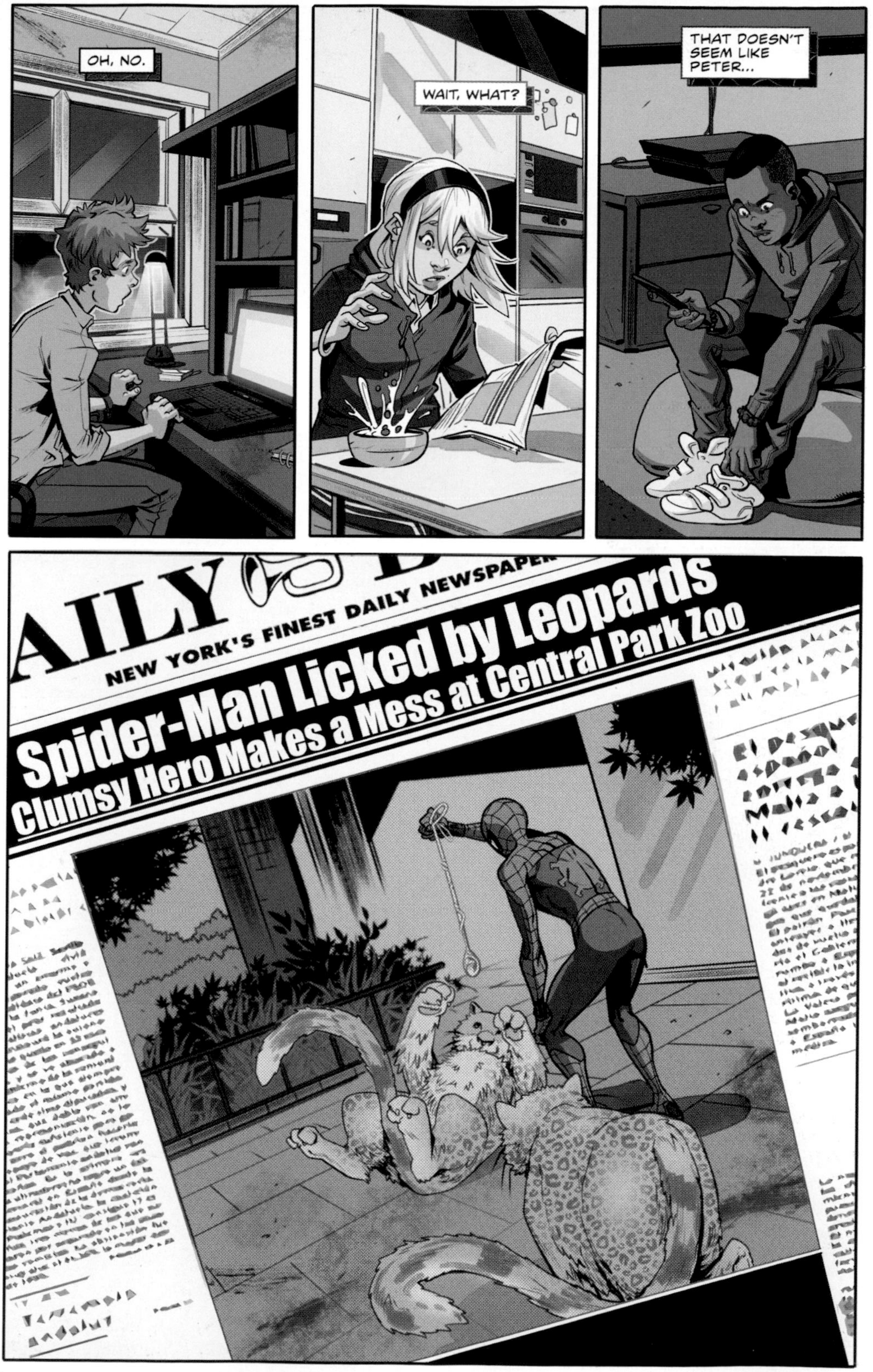
OH, NO.
WAIT, WHAT?
THAT DOESN'T SEEM LIKE PETER...
NEW YORK'S FINEST DAILY NEWSPAPE
Spider-Man Licked by Leopards
Clumsy Hero Makes a Mess at Central Park Zoo

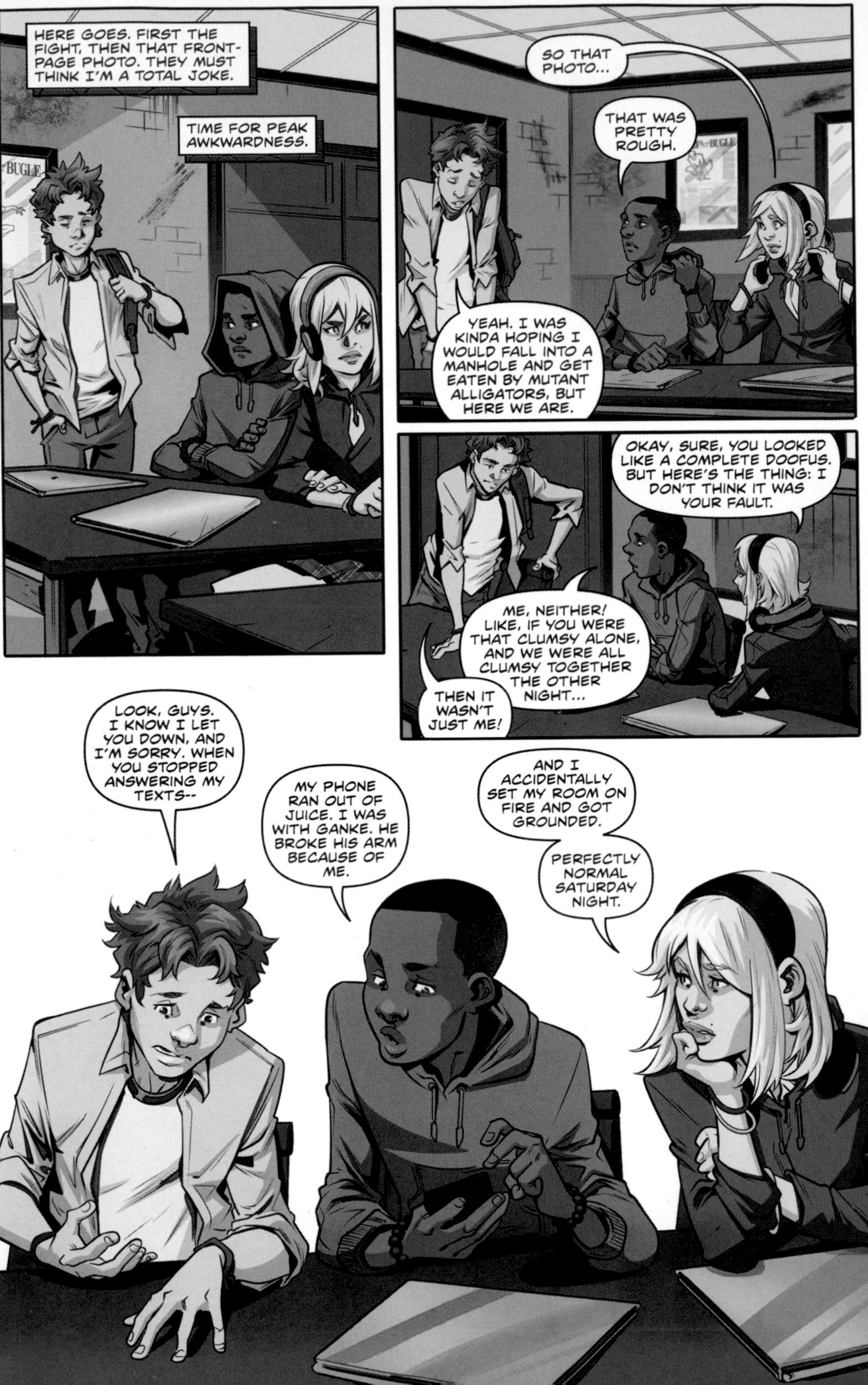
HERE GOES. FIRST THE FIGHT, THEN THAT FRONT-PAGE PHOTO. THEY MUST THINK I'M A TOTAL JOKE.
TIME FOR PEAK AWKWARDNESS.
BUGLE
SO THAT PHOTO...
THAT WAS PRETTY ROUGH.
YEAH. I WAS KINDA HOPING I WOULD FALL INTO A MANHOLE AND GET EATEN BY MUTANT ALLIGATORS, BUT HERE WE ARE.
OKAY, SURE, YOU LOOKED LIKE A COMPLETE DOOFUS. BUT HERE'S THE THING: I DON'T THINK IT WAS YOUR FAULT.
ME, NEITHER! LIKE, IF YOU WERE THAT CLUMSY ALONE, AND WE WERE ALL CLUMSY TOGETHER THE OTHER NIGHT...
THEN IT WASN'T JUST ME!
LOOK, GUYS. I KNOW I LET YOU DOWN, AND I'M SORRY. WHEN YOU STOPPED ANSWERING MY TEXTS--
MY PHONE RAN OUT OF JUICE. I WAS WITH GANKE. HE BROKE HIS ARM BECAUSE OF ME.
AND I ACCIDENTALLY SET MY ROOM ON FIRE AND GOT GROUNDED.
PERFECTLY NORMAL SATURDAY NIGHT.

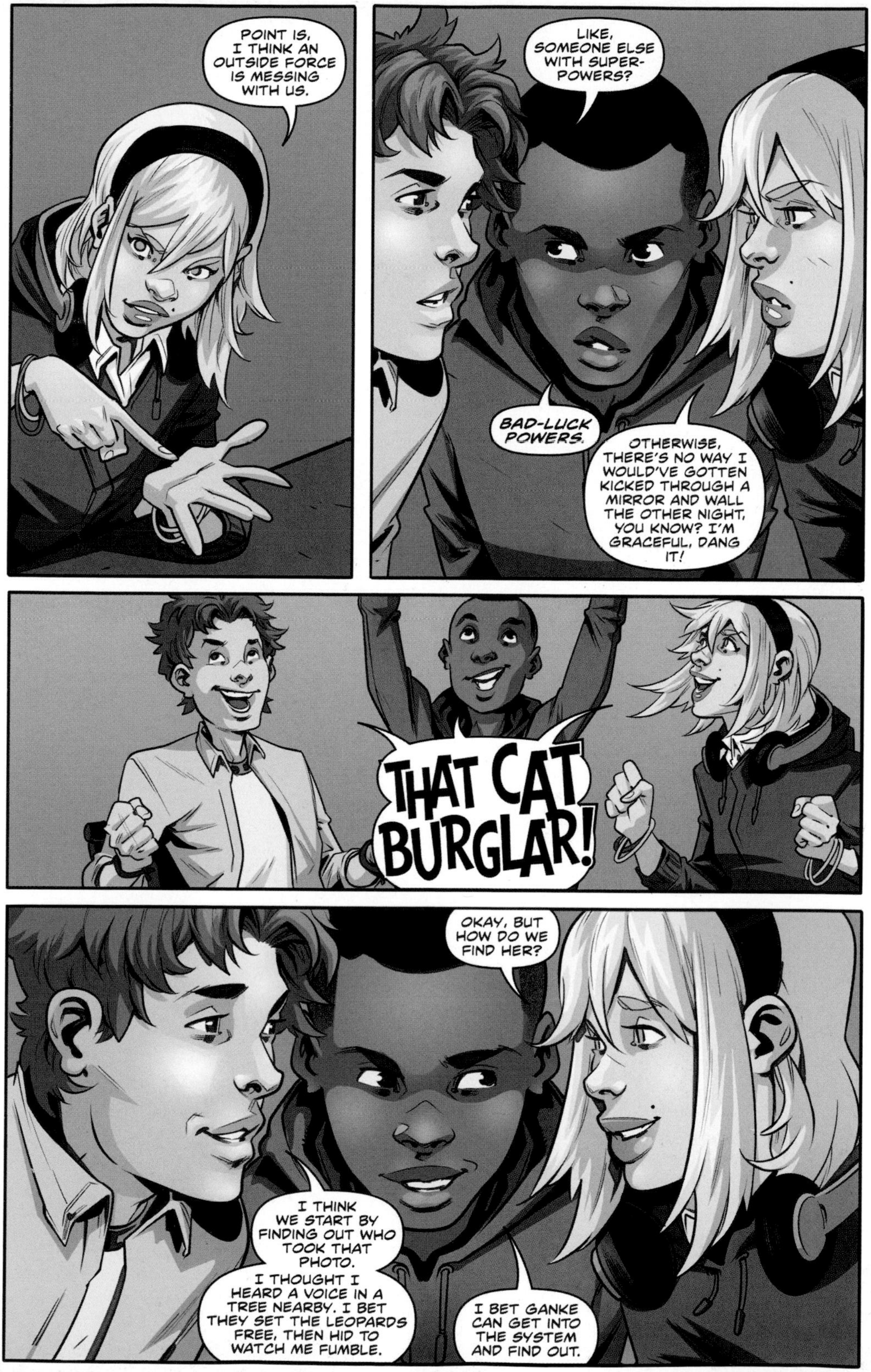
POINT IS, I THINK AN OUTSIDE FORCE IS MESSING WITH US.
LIKE, SOMEONE ELSE WITH SUPER-POWERS?
BAD-LUCK POWERS.
OTHERWISE, THERE'S NO WAY I WOULD'VE GOTTEN KICKED THROUGH A MIRROR AND WALL THE OTHER NIGHT, YOU KNOW? I'M GRACEFUL, DANG IT!
THAT CAT BURGLAR!
OKAY, BUT HOW DO WE FIND HER?
I THINK WE START BY FINDING OUT WHO TOOK THAT PHOTO.
I THOUGHT I HEARD A VOICE IN A TREE NEARBY. I BET THEY SET THE LEOPARDS FREE, THEN HID TO WATCH ME FUMBLE.
I BET GANKE CAN GET INTO THE SYSTEM AND FIND OUT.

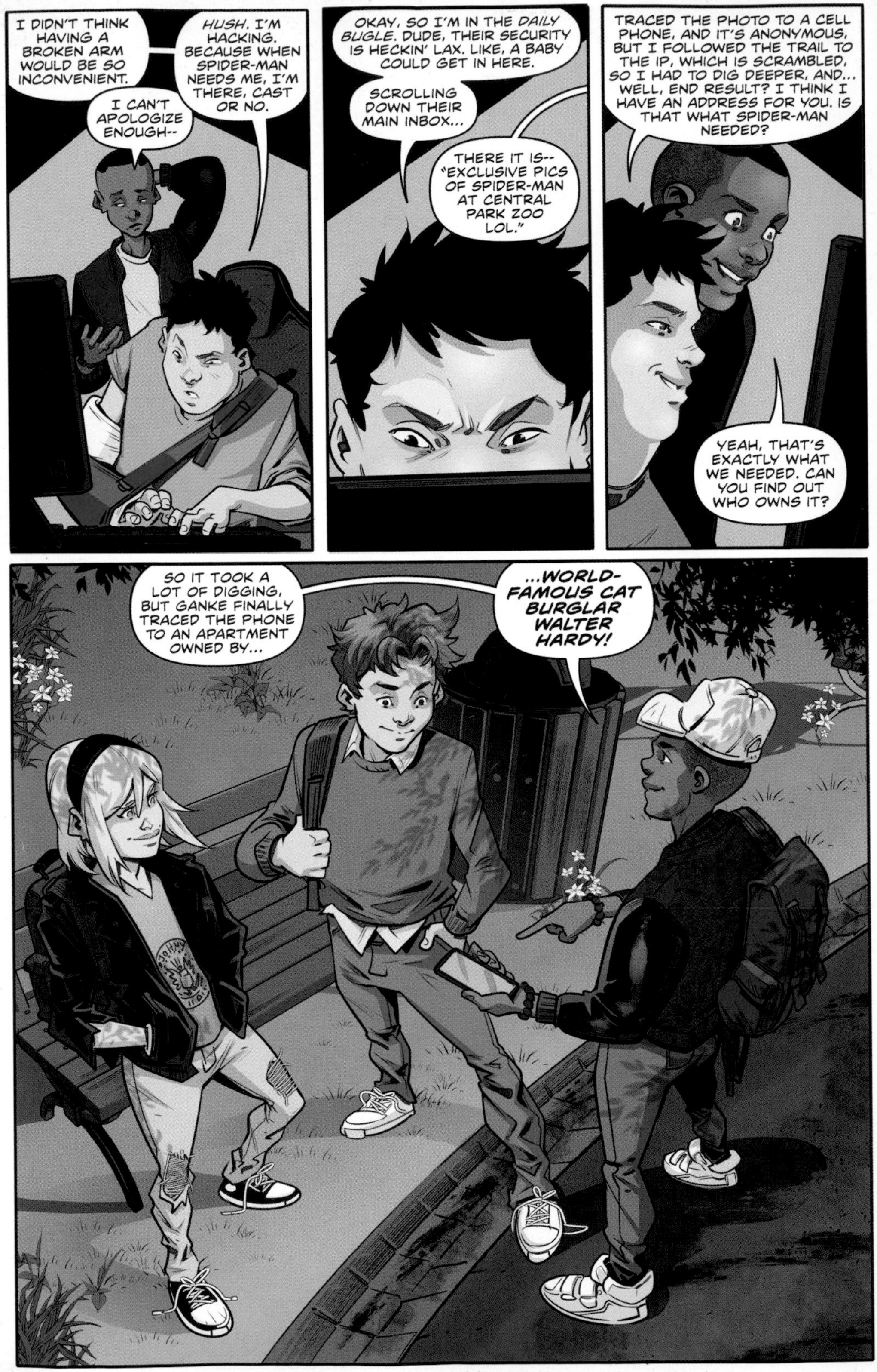
I DIDN'T THINK HAVING A BROKEN ARM WOULD BE SO INCONVENIENT.
HUSH. I'M HACKING. BECAUSE WHEN SPIDER-MAN NEEDS ME, I'M THERE, CAST OR NO.
I CAN'T APOLOGIZE ENOUGH--
OKAY, SO I'M IN THE *DAILY BUGLE*. DUDE, THEIR SECURITY IS HECKIN' LAX. LIKE, A BABY COULD GET IN HERE.
SCROLLING DOWN THEIR MAIN INBOX...
THERE IT IS-- "EXCLUSIVE PICS OF SPIDER-MAN AT CENTRAL PARK ZOO LOL."
TRACED THE PHOTO TO A CELL PHONE, AND IT'S ANONYMOUS, BUT I FOLLOWED THE TRAIL TO THE IP, WHICH IS SCRAMBLED, SO I HAD TO DIG DEEPER, AND... WELL, END RESULT? I THINK I HAVE AN ADDRESS FOR YOU. IS THAT WHAT SPIDER-MAN NEEDED?
YEAH, THAT'S EXACTLY WHAT WE NEEDED. CAN YOU FIND OUT WHO OWNS IT?
SO IT TOOK A LOT OF DIGGING, BUT GANKE FINALLY TRACED THE PHONE TO AN APARTMENT OWNED BY...
...WORLD-FAMOUS CAT BURGLAR WALTER HARDY!

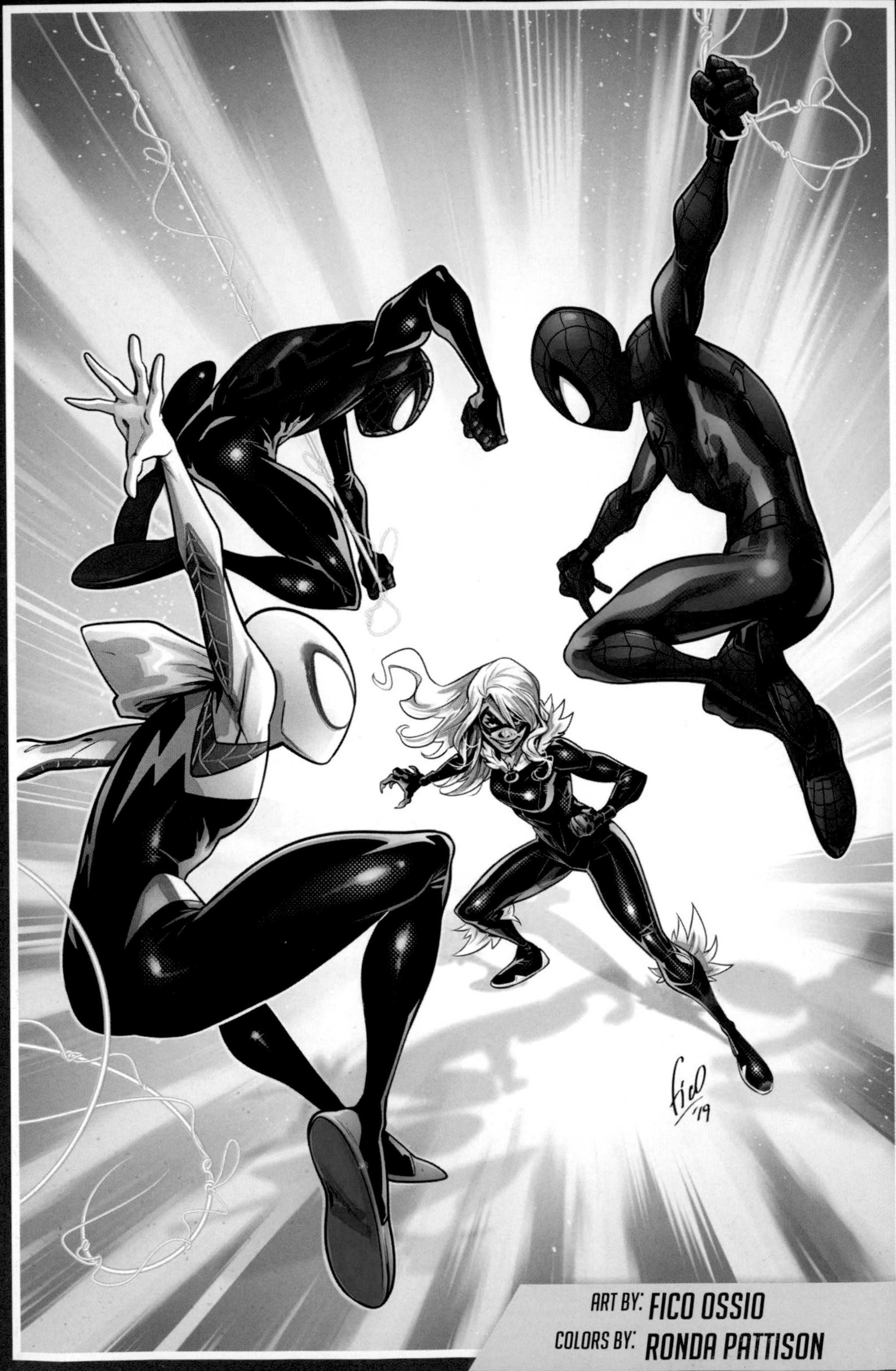

ART BY: FICO OSSIO
COLORS BY: RONDA PATTISON

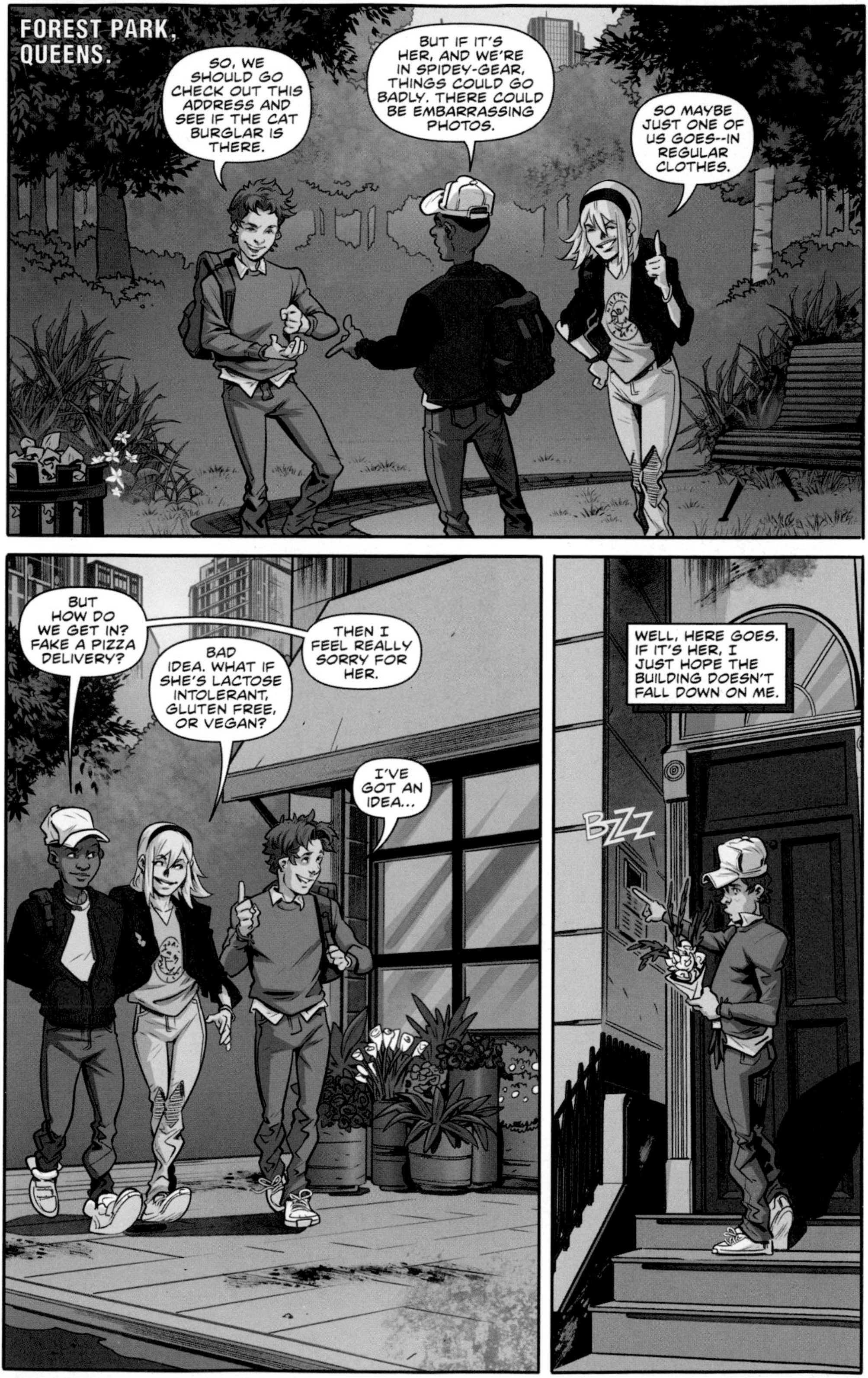
FOREST PARK, QUEENS.
SO, WE SHOULD GO CHECK OUT THIS ADDRESS AND SEE IF THE CAT BURGLAR IS THERE.
BUT IF IT'S HER, AND WE'RE IN SPIDEY-GEAR, THINGS COULD GO BADLY. THERE COULD BE EMBARRASSING PHOTOS.
SO MAYBE JUST ONE OF US GOES--IN REGULAR CLOTHES.
BUT HOW DO WE GET IN? FAKE A PIZZA DELIVERY?
BAD IDEA. WHAT IF SHE'S LACTOSE INTOLERANT, GLUTEN FREE, OR VEGAN?
THEN I FEEL REALLY SORRY FOR HER.
I'VE GOT AN IDEA...
WELL, HERE GOES. IF IT'S HER, I JUST HOPE THE BUILDING DOESN'T FALL DOWN ON ME.
BZZZ

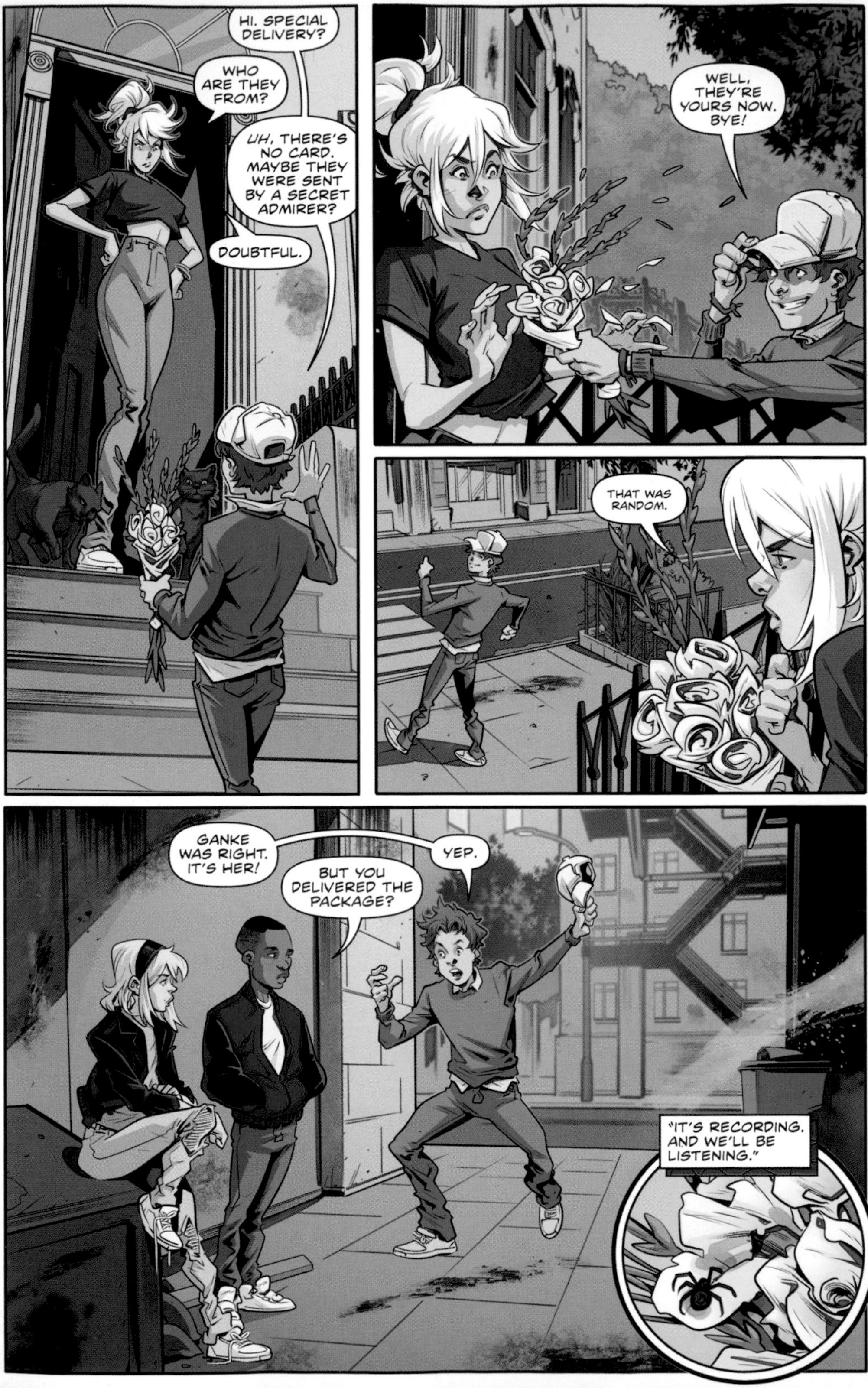
HI. SPECIAL DELIVERY?
WHO ARE THEY FROM?
UH, THERE'S NO CARD. MAYBE THEY WERE SENT BY A SECRET ADMIRER?
DOUBTFUL.
WELL, THEY'RE YOURS NOW. BYE!
THAT WAS RANDOM.
GANKE WAS RIGHT. IT'S HER!
YEP.
BUT YOU DELIVERED THE PACKAGE?
"IT'S RECORDING. AND WE'LL BE LISTENING."

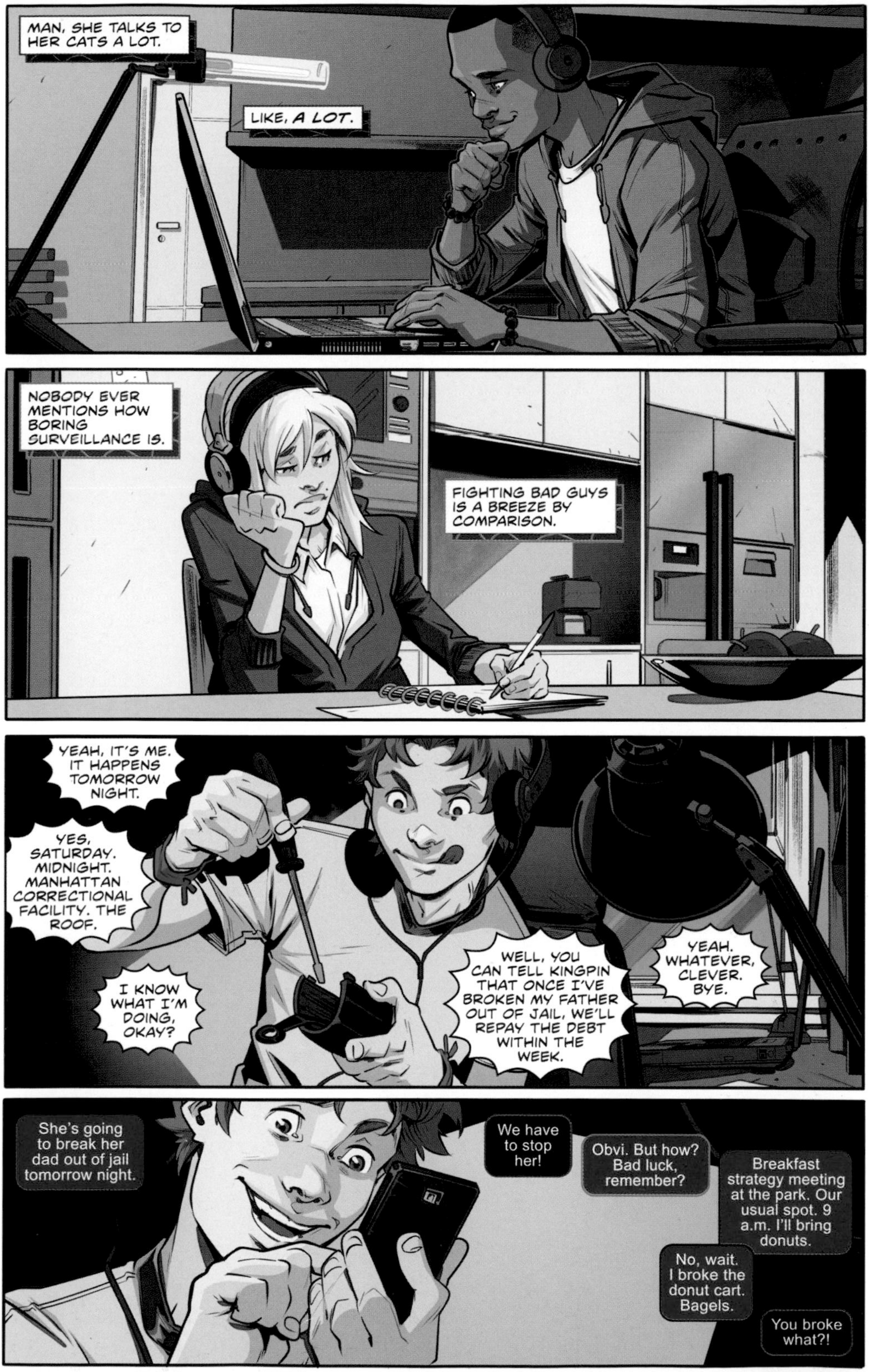
MAN, SHE TALKS TO HER CATS A LOT.
LIKE, A LOT.
NOBODY EVER MENTIONS HOW BORING SURVEILLANCE IS.
FIGHTING BAD GUYS IS A BREEZE BY COMPARISON.
YEAH, IT'S ME. IT HAPPENS TOMORROW NIGHT.
YES, SATURDAY. MIDNIGHT. MANHATTAN CORRECTIONAL FACILITY. THE ROOF.
I KNOW WHAT I'M DOING, OKAY?
WELL, YOU CAN TELL KINGPIN THAT ONCE I'VE BROKEN MY FATHER OUT OF JAIL, WE'LL REPAY THE DEBT WITHIN THE WEEK.
YEAH. WHATEVER, CLEVER. BYE.
She's going to break her dad out of jail tomorrow night.
We have to stop her!
Obvi. But how? Bad luck, remember?
Breakfast strategy meeting at the park. Our usual spot. 9 a.m. I'll bring donuts.
No, wait. I broke the donut cart. Bagels.
You broke what?!

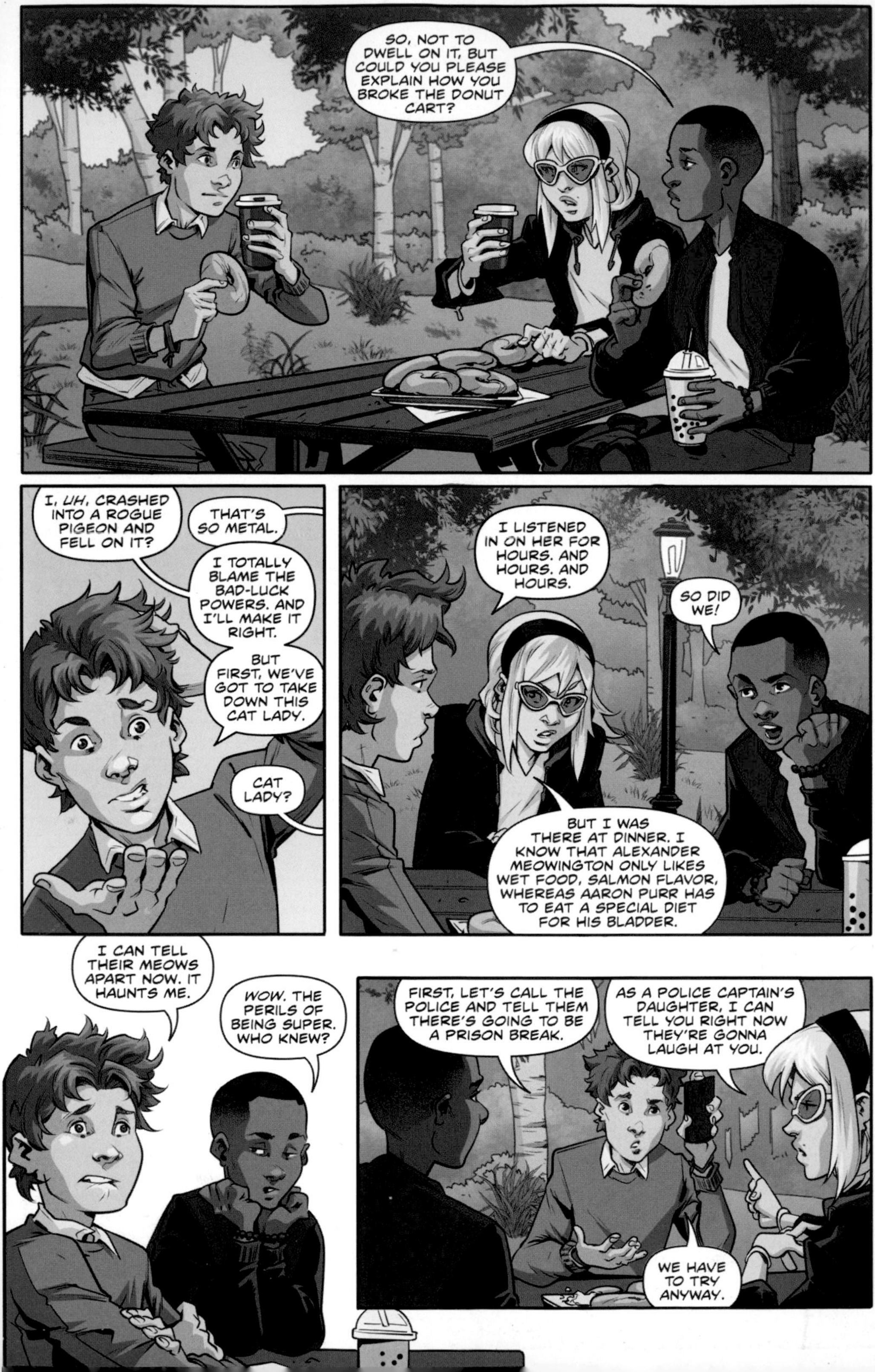
SO, NOT TO DWELL ON IT, BUT COULD YOU PLEASE EXPLAIN HOW YOU BROKE THE DONUT CART?
I, *UH*, CRASHED INTO A ROGUE PIGEON AND FELL ON IT?
THAT'S SO METAL.
I TOTALLY BLAME THE BAD-LUCK POWERS. AND I'LL MAKE IT RIGHT.
BUT FIRST, WE'VE GOT TO TAKE DOWN THIS CAT LADY.
CAT LADY?
I LISTENED IN ON HER FOR HOURS. AND HOURS. AND HOURS.
SO DID WE!
BUT I WAS THERE AT DINNER. I KNOW THAT ALEXANDER MEOWINGTON ONLY LIKES WET FOOD, SALMON FLAVOR, WHEREAS AARON PURR HAS TO EAT A SPECIAL DIET FOR HIS BLADDER.
I CAN TELL THEIR MEOWS APART NOW. IT HAUNTS ME.
WOW. THE PERILS OF BEING SUPER. WHO KNEW?
FIRST, LET'S CALL THE POLICE AND TELL THEM THERE'S GOING TO BE A PRISON BREAK.
AS A POLICE CAPTAIN'S DAUGHTER, I CAN TELL YOU RIGHT NOW THEY'RE GONNA LAUGH AT YOU.
WE HAVE TO TRY ANYWAY.

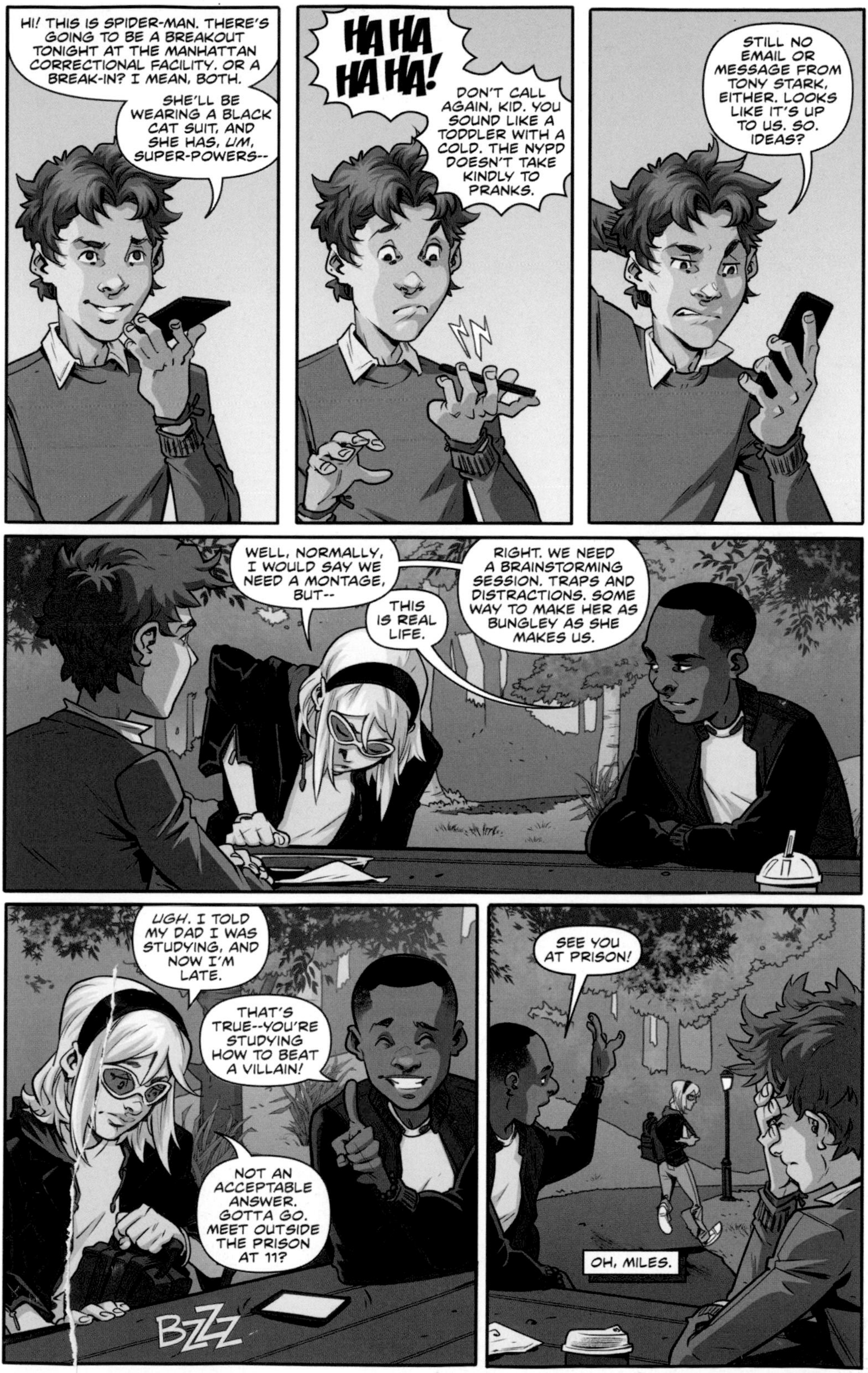
HI! THIS IS SPIDER-MAN. THERE'S GOING TO BE A BREAKOUT TONIGHT AT THE MANHATTAN CORRECTIONAL FACILITY. OR A BREAK-IN? I MEAN, BOTH.
SHE'LL BE WEARING A BLACK CAT SUIT, AND SHE HAS, UM, SUPER-POWERS--
HA HA HA HA!
DON'T CALL AGAIN, KID. YOU SOUND LIKE A TODDLER WITH A COLD. THE NYPD DOESN'T TAKE KINDLY TO PRANKS.
STILL NO EMAIL OR MESSAGE FROM TONY STARK, EITHER. LOOKS LIKE IT'S UP TO US. SO. IDEAS?
WELL, NORMALLY, I WOULD SAY WE NEED A MONTAGE, BUT--
THIS IS REAL LIFE.
RIGHT. WE NEED A BRAINSTORMING SESSION. TRAPS AND DISTRACTIONS. SOME WAY TO MAKE HER AS BUNGLEY AS SHE MAKES US.
UGH. I TOLD MY DAD I WAS STUDYING, AND NOW I'M LATE.
THAT'S TRUE--YOU'RE STUDYING HOW TO BEAT A VILLAIN!
NOT AN ACCEPTABLE ANSWER. GOTTA GO. MEET OUTSIDE THE PRISON AT 11?
BZZZ
SEE YOU AT PRISON!
OH, MILES.

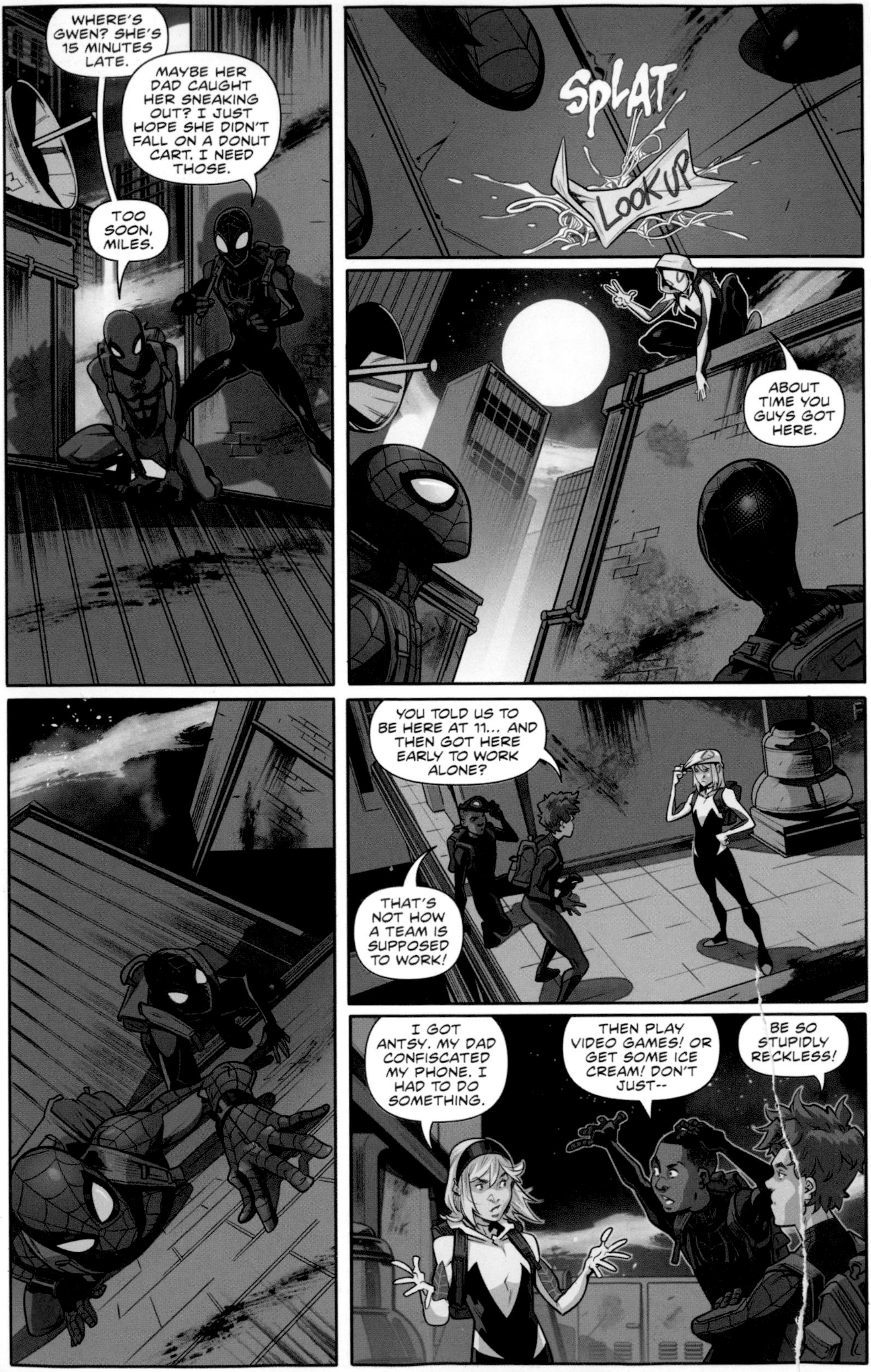
WHERE'S GWEN? SHE'S 15 MINUTES LATE.
MAYBE HER DAD CAUGHT HER SNEAKING OUT? I JUST HOPE SHE DIDN'T FALL ON A DONUT CART. I NEED THOSE.
TOO SOON, MILES.
SPLAT
LOOK UP
ABOUT TIME YOU GUYS GOT HERE.
YOU TOLD US TO BE HERE AT 11... AND THEN GOT HERE EARLY TO WORK ALONE?
THAT'S NOT HOW A TEAM IS SUPPOSED TO WORK!
I GOT ANTSY. MY DAD CONFISCATED MY PHONE. I HAD TO DO SOMETHING.
THEN PLAY VIDEO GAMES! OR GET SOME ICE CREAM! DON'T JUST--
BE SO STUPIDLY RECKLESS!

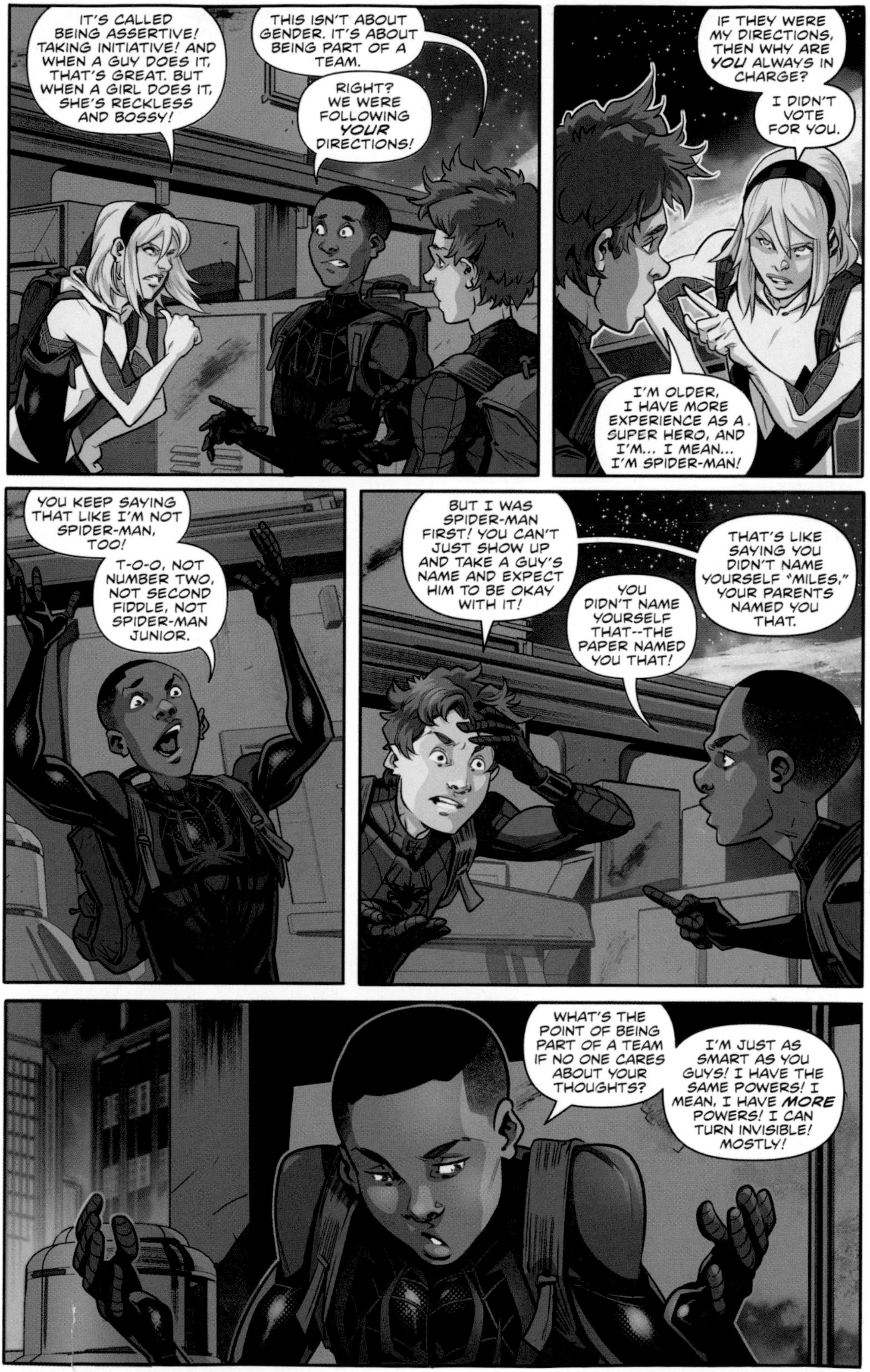
IT'S CALLED BEING ASSERTIVE! TAKING INITIATIVE! AND WHEN A GUY DOES IT, THAT'S GREAT. BUT WHEN A GIRL DOES IT, SHE'S RECKLESS AND BOSSY!
THIS ISN'T ABOUT GENDER. IT'S ABOUT BEING PART OF A TEAM.
RIGHT? WE WERE FOLLOWING YOUR DIRECTIONS!
IF THEY WERE MY DIRECTIONS, THEN WHY ARE YOU ALWAYS IN CHARGE?
I DIDN'T VOTE FOR YOU.
I'M OLDER, I HAVE MORE EXPERIENCE AS A SUPER HERO, AND I'M... I MEAN... I'M SPIDER-MAN!
YOU KEEP SAYING THAT LIKE I'M NOT SPIDER-MAN, TOO!
T-O-O, NOT NUMBER TWO, NOT SECOND FIDDLE, NOT SPIDER-MAN JUNIOR.
BUT I WAS SPIDER-MAN FIRST! YOU CAN'T JUST SHOW UP AND TAKE A GUY'S NAME AND EXPECT HIM TO BE OKAY WITH IT!
YOU DIDN'T NAME YOURSELF THAT--THE PAPER NAMED YOU THAT!
THAT'S LIKE SAYING YOU DIDN'T NAME YOURSELF "MILES," YOUR PARENTS NAMED YOU THAT.
WHAT'S THE POINT OF BEING PART OF A TEAM IF NO ONE CARES ABOUT YOUR THOUGHTS?
I'M JUST AS SMART AS YOU GUYS! I HAVE THE SAME POWERS! I MEAN, I HAVE MORE POWERS! I CAN TURN INVISIBLE! MOSTLY!

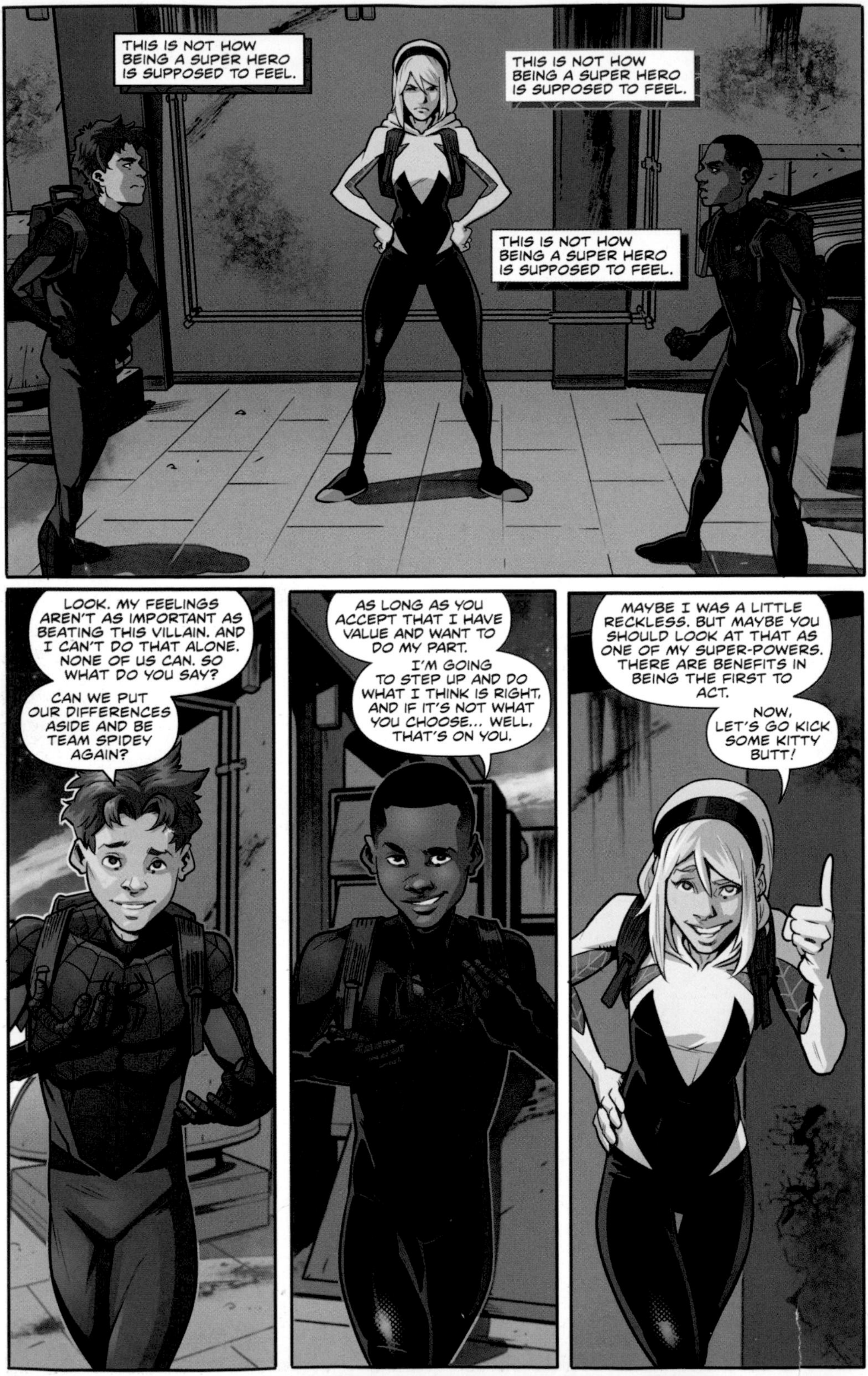

THIS IS NOT HOW BEING A SUPER HERO IS SUPPOSED TO FEEL.
THIS IS NOT HOW BEING A SUPER HERO IS SUPPOSED TO FEEL.
THIS IS NOT HOW BEING A SUPER HERO IS SUPPOSED TO FEEL.
LOOK. MY FEELINGS AREN'T AS IMPORTANT AS BEATING THIS VILLAIN. AND I CAN'T DO THAT ALONE. NONE OF US CAN. SO WHAT DO YOU SAY?
CAN WE PUT OUR DIFFERENCES ASIDE AND BE TEAM SPIDEY AGAIN?
AS LONG AS YOU ACCEPT THAT I HAVE VALUE AND WANT TO DO MY PART.
I'M GOING TO STEP UP AND DO WHAT I THINK IS RIGHT, AND IF IT'S NOT WHAT YOU CHOOSE... WELL, THAT'S ON YOU.
MAYBE I WAS A LITTLE RECKLESS. BUT MAYBE YOU SHOULD LOOK AT THAT AS ONE OF MY SUPER-POWERS. THERE ARE BENEFITS IN BEING THE FIRST TO ACT.
NOW, LET'S GO KICK SOME KITTY BUTT!

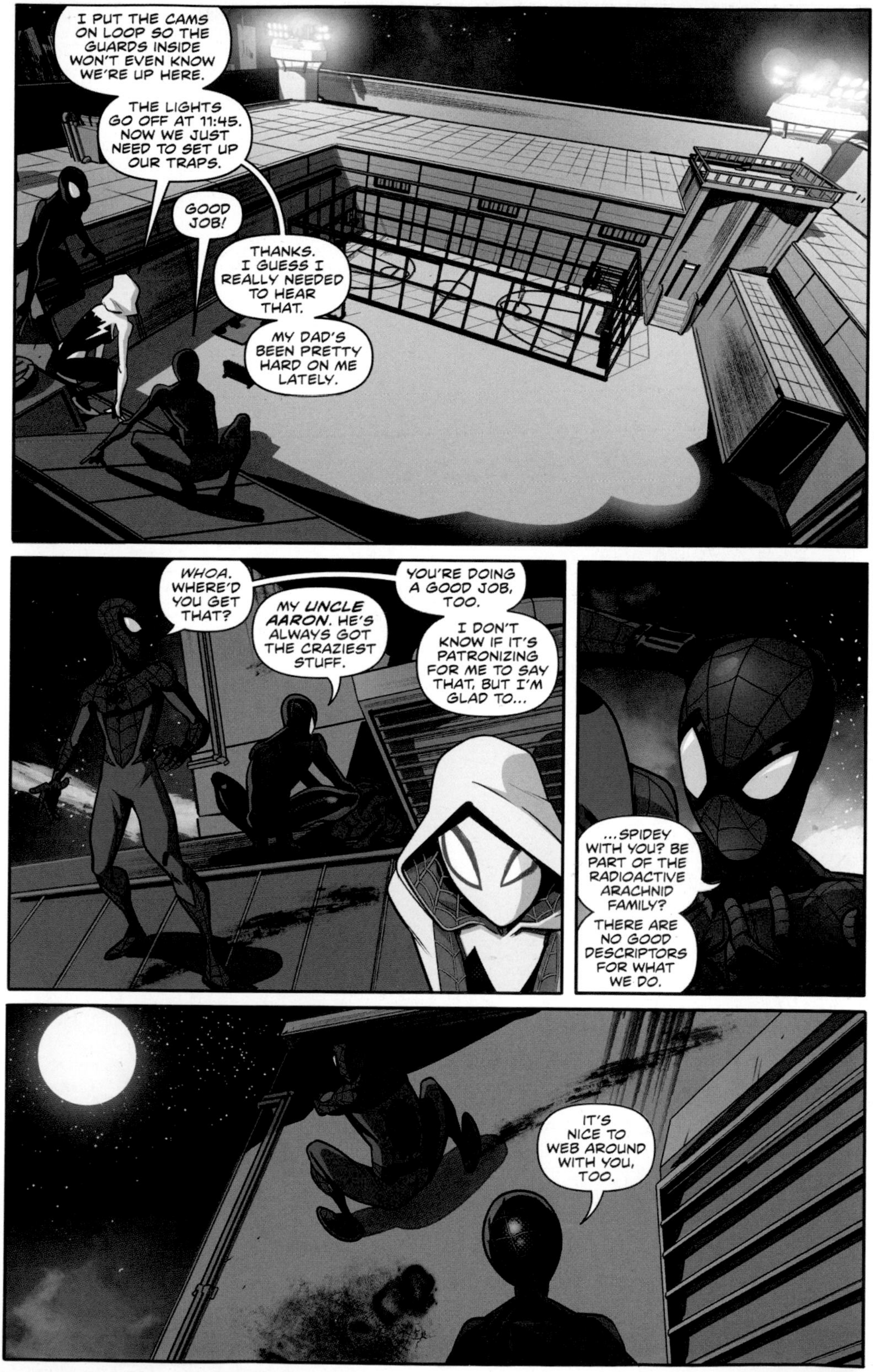
I PUT THE CAMS ON LOOP SO THE GUARDS INSIDE WON'T EVEN KNOW WE'RE UP HERE.
THE LIGHTS GO OFF AT 11:45. NOW WE JUST NEED TO SET UP OUR TRAPS.
GOOD JOB!
THANKS. I GUESS I REALLY NEEDED TO HEAR THAT.
MY DAD'S BEEN PRETTY HARD ON ME LATELY.
WHOA. WHERE'D YOU GET THAT?
MY *UNCLE AARON*. HE'S ALWAYS GOT THE CRAZIEST STUFF.
YOU'RE DOING A GOOD JOB, TOO.
I DON'T KNOW IF IT'S PATRONIZING FOR ME TO SAY THAT, BUT I'M GLAD TO...
...SPIDEY WITH YOU? BE PART OF THE RADIOACTIVE ARACHNID FAMILY?
THERE ARE NO GOOD DESCRIPTORS FOR WHAT WE DO.
IT'S NICE TO WEB AROUND WITH YOU, TOO.

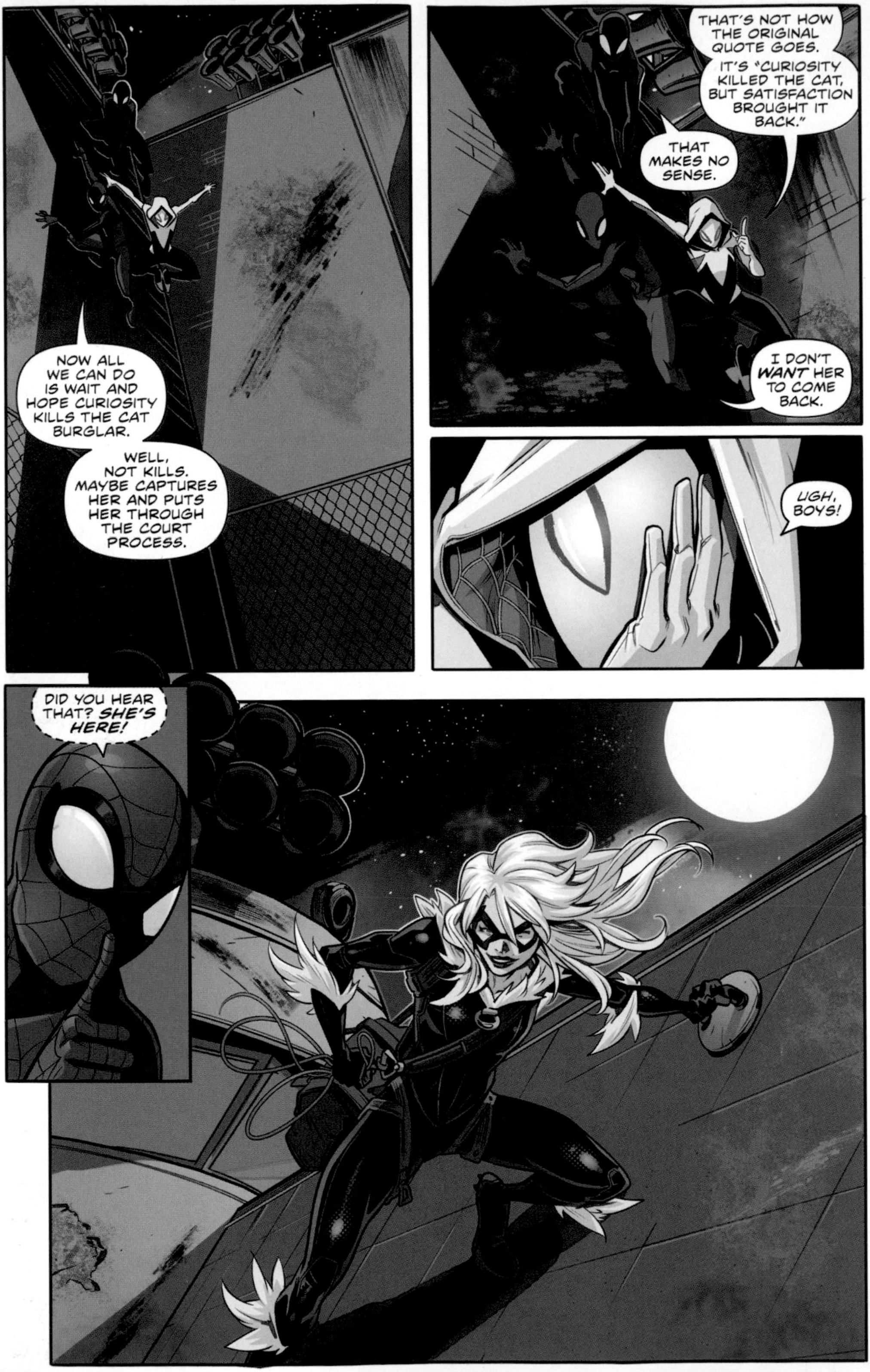
NOW ALL WE CAN DO IS WAIT AND HOPE CURIOSITY KILLS THE CAT BURGLAR.
WELL, NOT KILLS. MAYBE CAPTURES HER AND PUTS HER THROUGH THE COURT PROCESS.
THAT'S NOT HOW THE ORIGINAL QUOTE GOES.
IT'S "CURIOSITY KILLED THE CAT, BUT SATISFACTION BROUGHT IT BACK."
THAT MAKES NO SENSE.
I DON'T *WANT* HER TO COME BACK.
UGH, BOYS!
DID YOU HEAR THAT? *SHE'S HERE!*

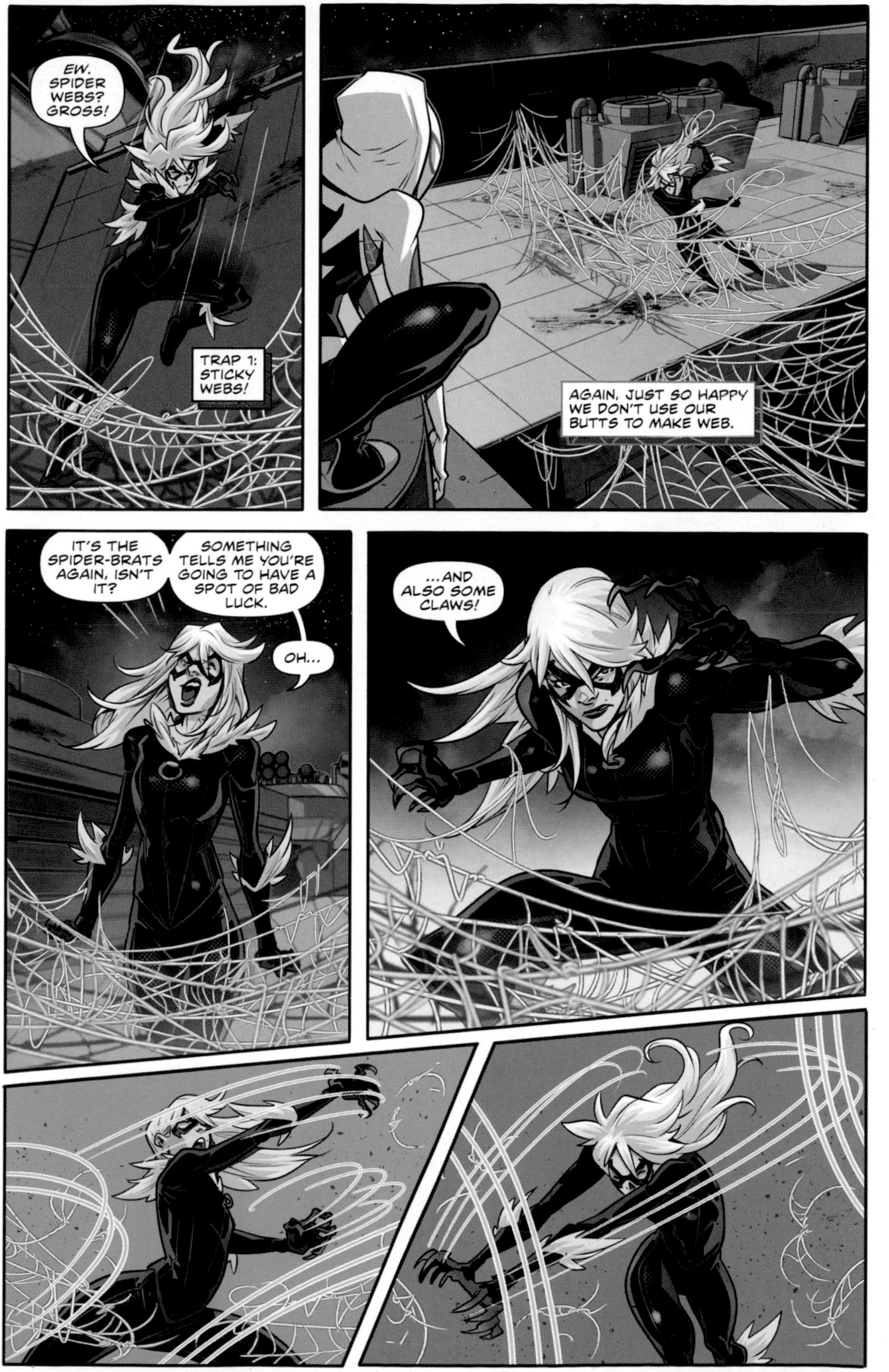
EW. SPIDER WEBS? GROSS!
TRAP 1: STICKY WEBS!
AGAIN, JUST SO HAPPY WE DON'T USE OUR BUTTS TO MAKE WEB.
IT'S THE SPIDER-BRATS AGAIN, ISN'T IT?
SOMETHING TELLS ME YOU'RE GOING TO HAVE A SPOT OF BAD LUCK.
OH...
...AND ALSO SOME CLAWS!

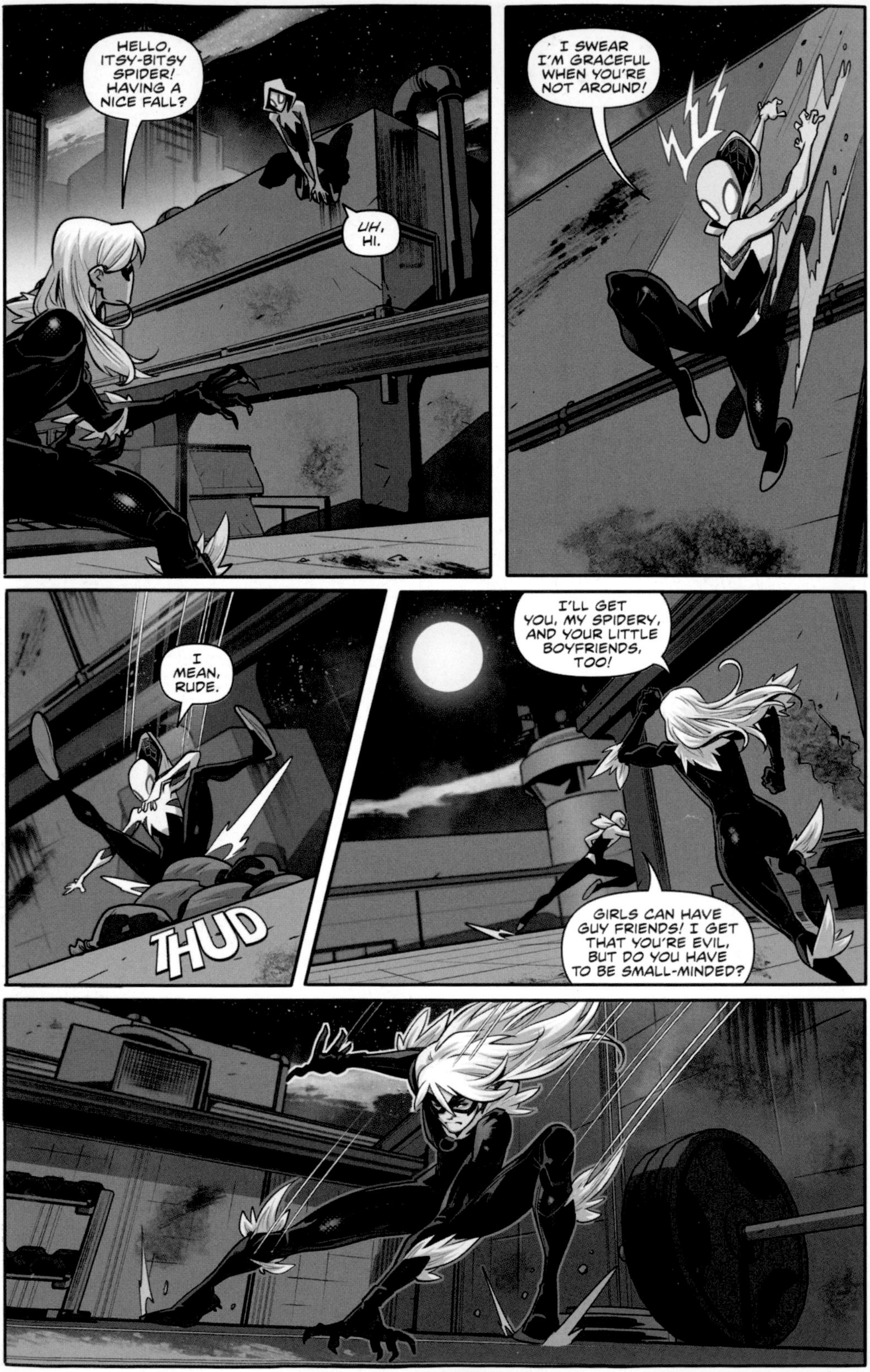
HELLO, ITSY-BITSY SPIDER! HAVING A NICE FALL?
UH, HI.
I SWEAR I'M GRACEFUL WHEN YOU'RE NOT AROUND!
I MEAN, RUDE.
THUD
I'LL GET YOU, MY SPIDERY, AND YOUR LITTLE BOYFRIENDS, TOO!
GIRLS CAN HAVE GUY FRIENDS! I GET THAT YOU'RE EVIL, BUT DO YOU HAVE TO BE SMALL-MINDED?

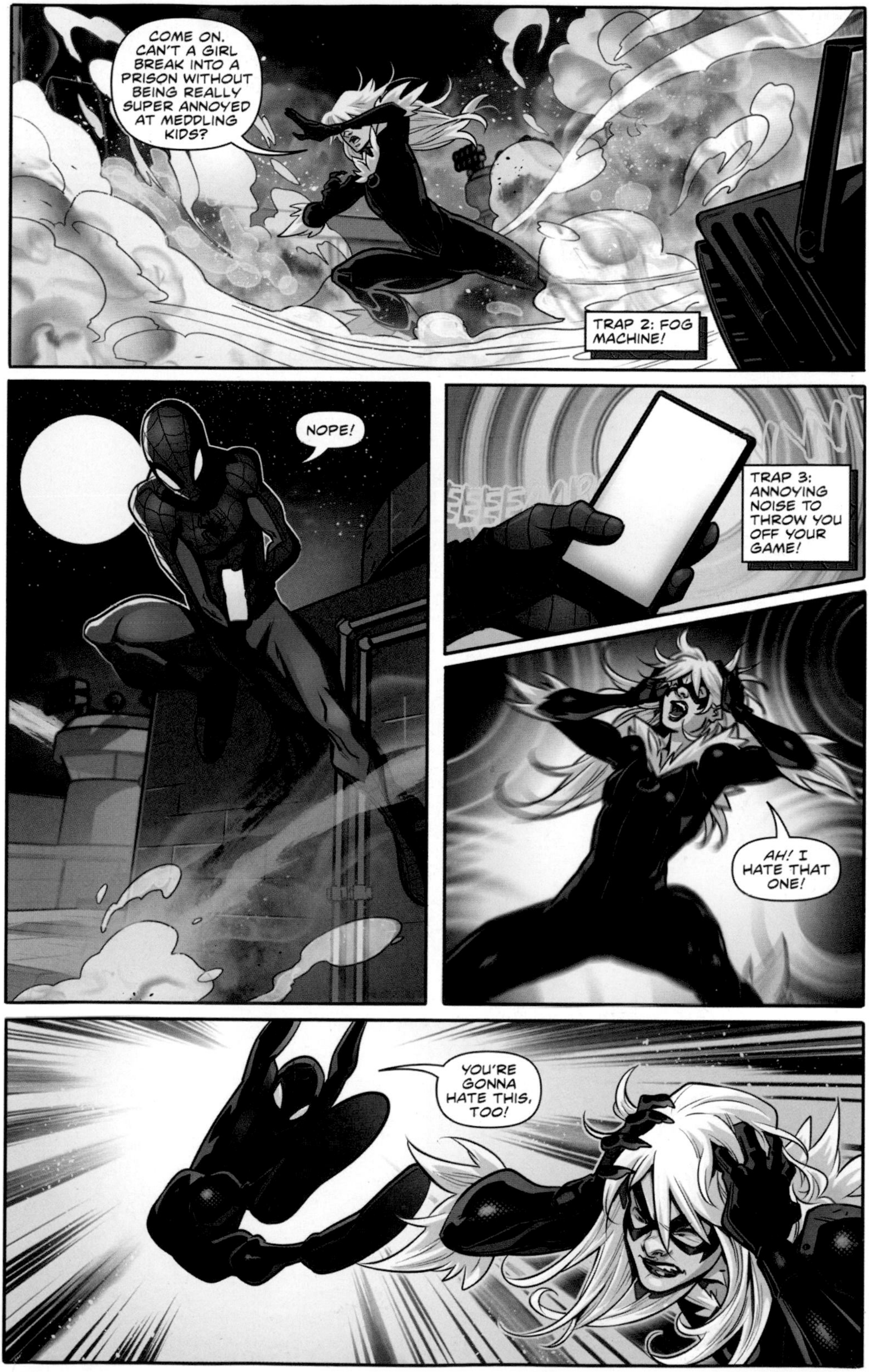
COME ON. CAN'T A GIRL BREAK INTO A PRISON WITHOUT BEING REALLY SUPER ANNOYED AT MEDDLING KIDS?
TRAP 2: FOG MACHINE!
NOPE!
TRAP 3: ANNOYING NOISE TO THROW YOU OFF YOUR GAME!
AH! I HATE THAT ONE!
YOU'RE GONNA HATE THIS, TOO!

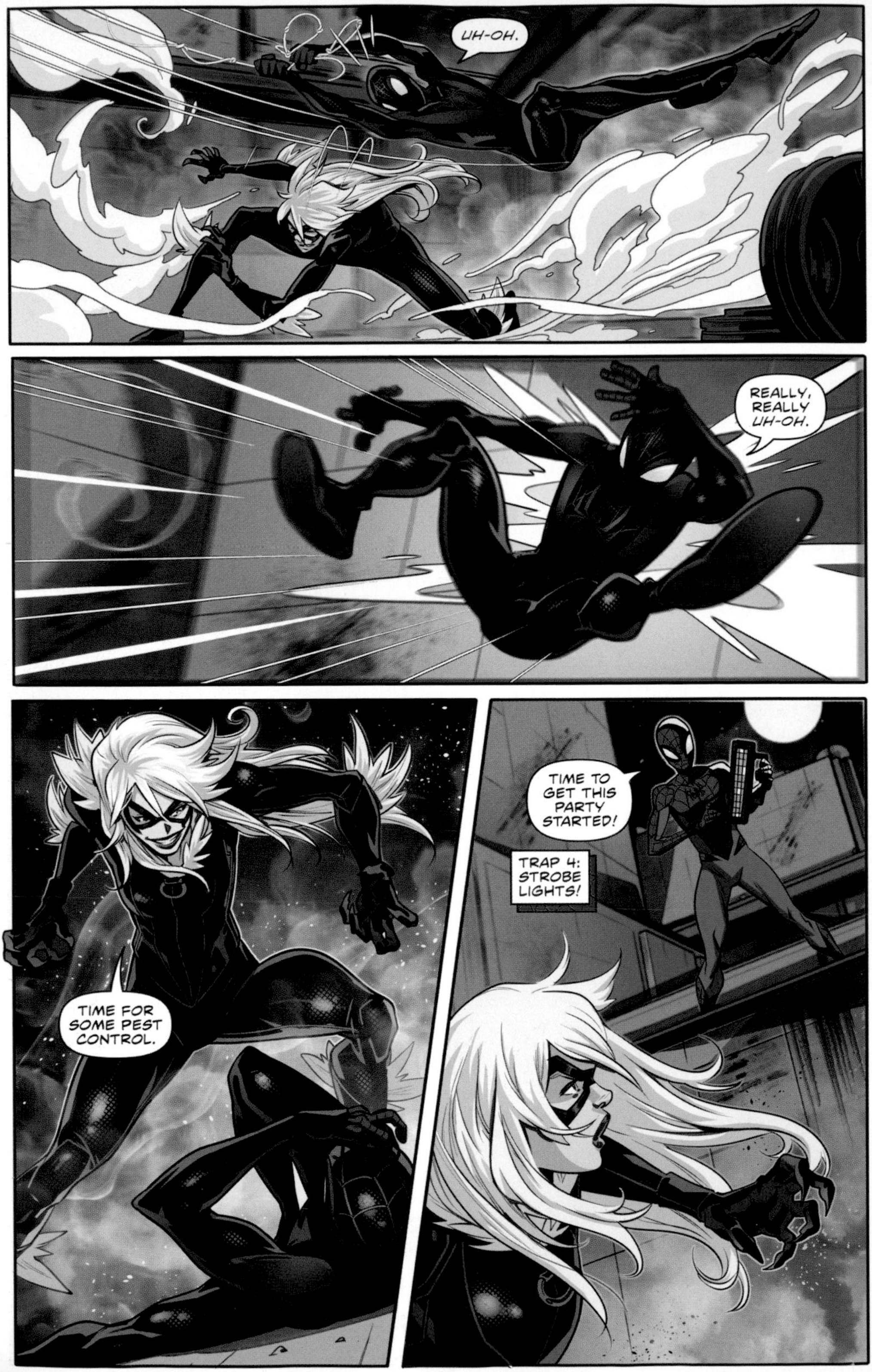
UH-OH.
REALLY, REALLY UH-OH.
TIME FOR SOME PEST CONTROL.
TIME TO GET THIS PARTY STARTED!
TRAP 4: STROBE LIGHTS!

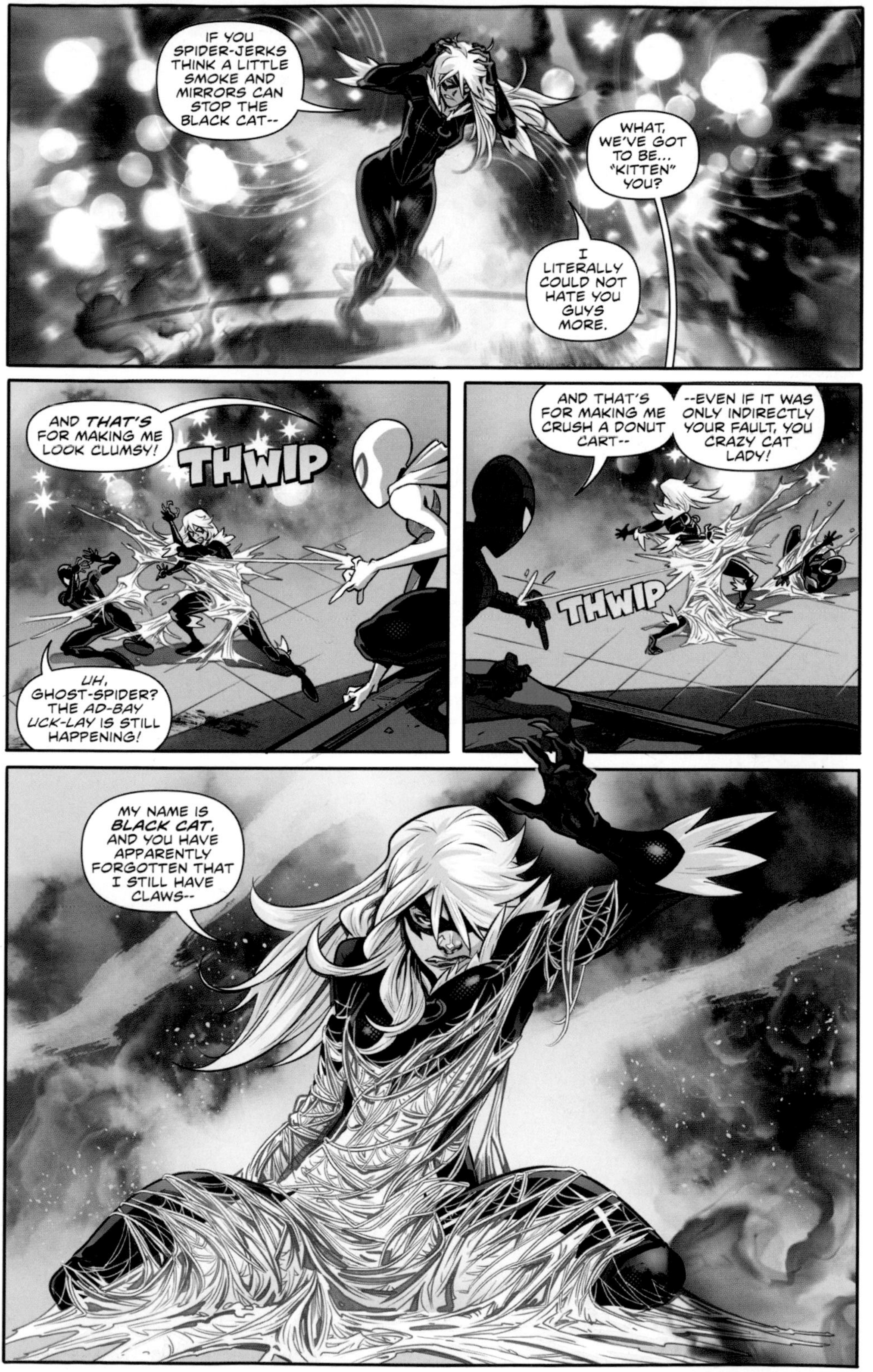
IF YOU SPIDER-JERKS THINK A LITTLE SMOKE AND MIRRORS CAN STOP THE BLACK CAT--
WHAT, WE'VE GOT TO BE... "KITTEN" YOU?
I LITERALLY COULD NOT HATE YOU GUYS MORE.
AND *THAT'S* FOR MAKING ME LOOK CLUMSY!
THWIP
UH, GHOST-SPIDER? THE AD-BAY UCK-LAY IS STILL HAPPENING!
AND THAT'S FOR MAKING ME CRUSH A DONUT CART--
--EVEN IF IT WAS ONLY INDIRECTLY YOUR FAULT, YOU CRAZY CAT LADY!
THWIP
MY NAME IS *BLACK CAT*, AND YOU HAVE APPARENTLY FORGOTTEN THAT I STILL HAVE CLAWS--

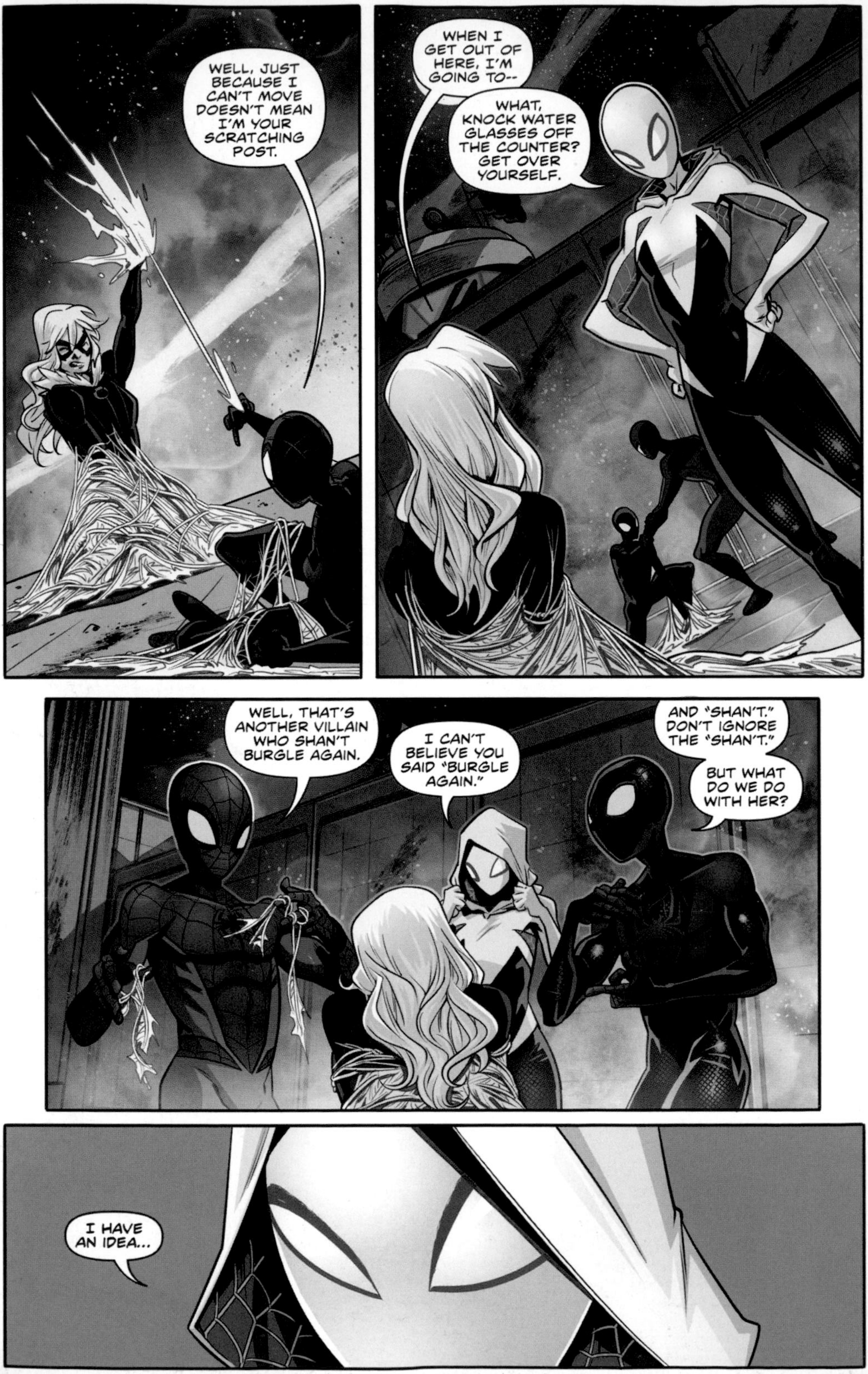
WELL, JUST BECAUSE I CAN'T MOVE DOESN'T MEAN I'M YOUR SCRATCHING POST.
WHEN I GET OUT OF HERE, I'M GOING TO--
WHAT, KNOCK WATER GLASSES OFF THE COUNTER? GET OVER YOURSELF.
WELL, THAT'S ANOTHER VILLAIN WHO SHAN'T BURGLE AGAIN.
I CAN'T BELIEVE YOU SAID "BURGLE AGAIN."
AND "SHAN'T." DON'T IGNORE THE "SHAN'T."
BUT WHAT DO WE DO WITH HER?
I HAVE AN IDEA...

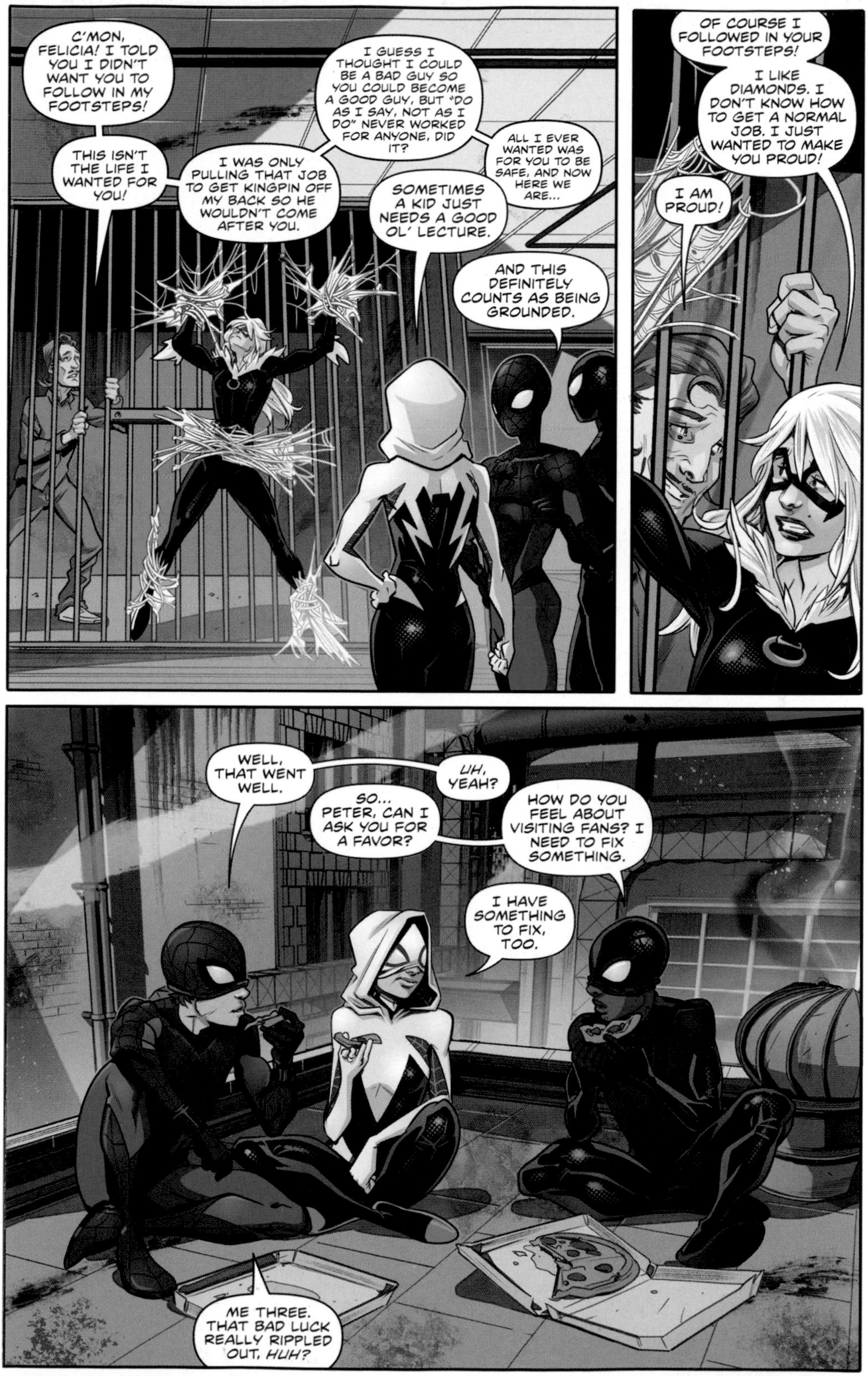
C'MON, FELICIA! I TOLD YOU I DIDN'T WANT YOU TO FOLLOW IN MY FOOTSTEPS!
THIS ISN'T THE LIFE I WANTED FOR YOU!
I WAS ONLY PULLING THAT JOB TO GET KINGPIN OFF MY BACK SO HE WOULDN'T COME AFTER YOU.
I GUESS I THOUGHT I COULD BE A BAD GUY SO YOU COULD BECOME A GOOD GUY, BUT "DO AS I SAY, NOT AS I DO" NEVER WORKED FOR ANYONE, DID IT?
ALL I EVER WANTED WAS FOR YOU TO BE SAFE, AND NOW HERE WE ARE...
SOMETIMES A KID JUST NEEDS A GOOD OL' LECTURE.
AND THIS DEFINITELY COUNTS AS BEING GROUNDED.
OF COURSE I FOLLOWED IN YOUR FOOTSTEPS!
I LIKE DIAMONDS. I DON'T KNOW HOW TO GET A NORMAL JOB. I JUST WANTED TO MAKE YOU PROUD!
I AM PROUD!
WELL, THAT WENT WELL.
UH, YEAH?
SO... PETER, CAN I ASK YOU FOR A FAVOR?
HOW DO YOU FEEL ABOUT VISITING FANS? I NEED TO FIX SOMETHING.
I HAVE SOMETHING TO FIX, TOO.
ME THREE. THAT BAD LUCK REALLY RIPPLED OUT, HUH?

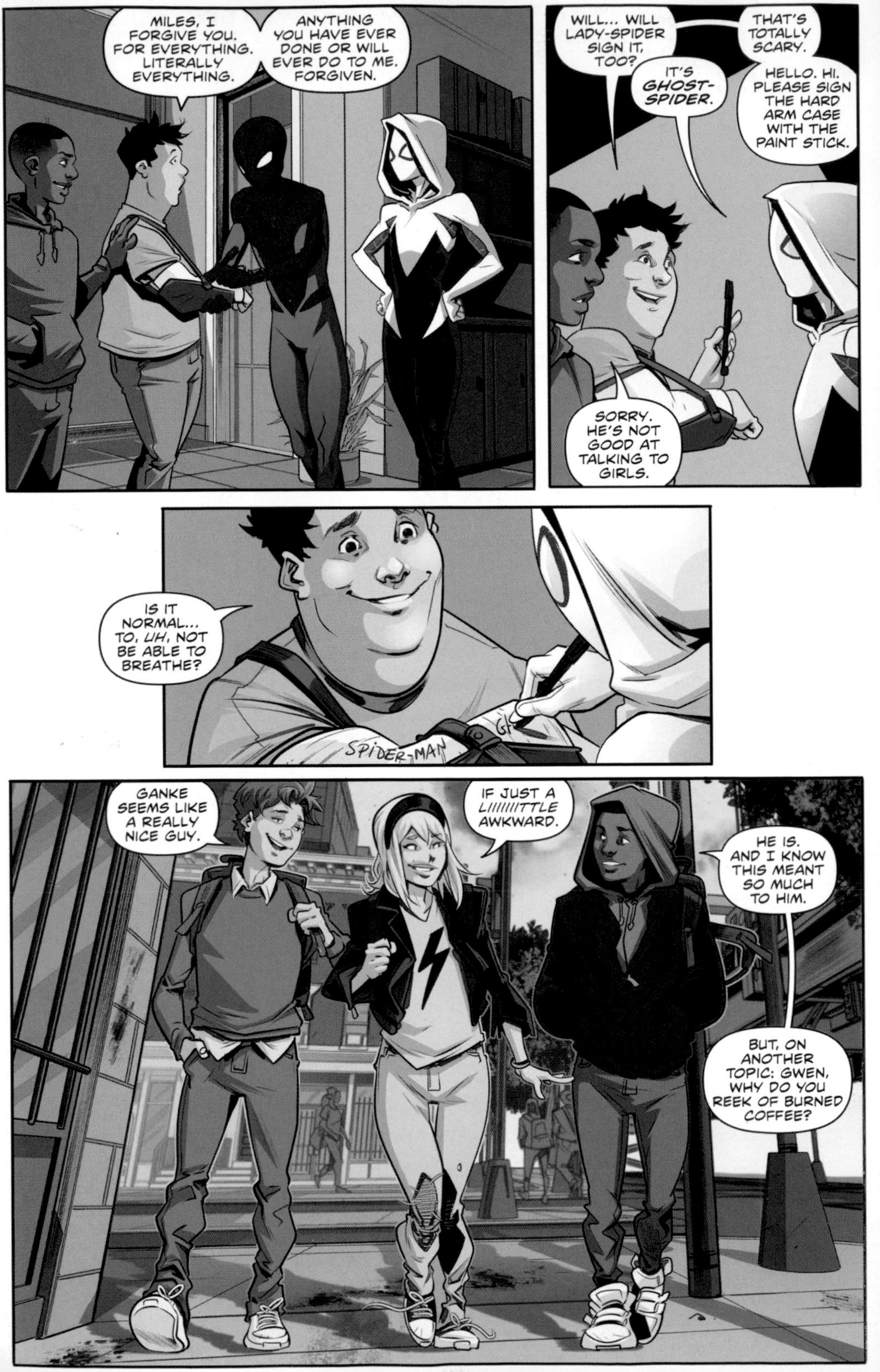
MILES, I FORGIVE YOU. FOR EVERYTHING. LITERALLY EVERYTHING.
ANYTHING YOU HAVE EVER DONE OR WILL EVER DO TO ME. FORGIVEN.
WILL... WILL LADY-SPIDER SIGN IT, TOO?
THAT'S TOTALLY SCARY.
IT'S *GHOST-SPIDER*.
HELLO. HI. PLEASE SIGN THE HARD ARM CASE WITH THE PAINT STICK.
SORRY. HE'S NOT GOOD AT TALKING TO GIRLS.
IS IT NORMAL... TO, *UH*, NOT BE ABLE TO BREATHE?
SPIDER-MAN
GANKE SEEMS LIKE A REALLY NICE GUY.
IF JUST A *LIIIIIIITTLE* AWKWARD.
HE IS. AND I KNOW THIS MEANT SO MUCH TO HIM.
BUT, ON ANOTHER TOPIC: GWEN, WHY DO YOU REEK OF BURNED COFFEE?

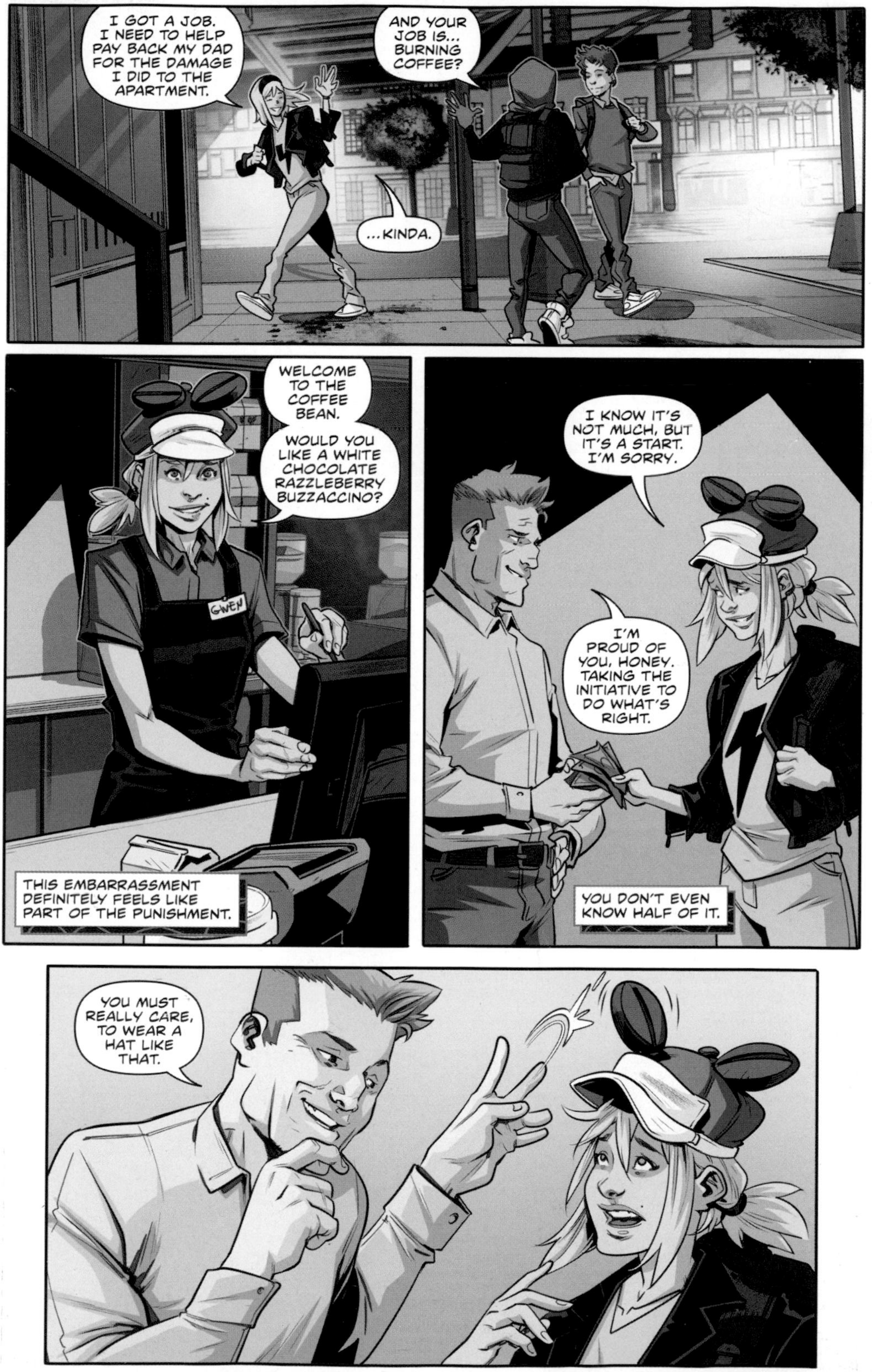

I GOT A JOB. I NEED TO HELP PAY BACK MY DAD FOR THE DAMAGE I DID TO THE APARTMENT.
AND YOUR JOB IS... BURNING COFFEE?
...KINDA.
WELCOME TO THE COFFEE BEAN.
WOULD YOU LIKE A WHITE CHOCOLATE RAZZLEBERRY BUZZACCINO?
GWEN
THIS EMBARRASSMENT DEFINITELY FEELS LIKE PART OF THE PUNISHMENT.
I KNOW IT'S NOT MUCH, BUT IT'S A START. I'M SORRY.
I'M PROUD OF YOU, HONEY. TAKING THE INITIATIVE TO DO WHAT'S RIGHT.
YOU DON'T EVEN KNOW HALF OF IT.
YOU MUST REALLY CARE, TO WEAR A HAT LIKE THAT.

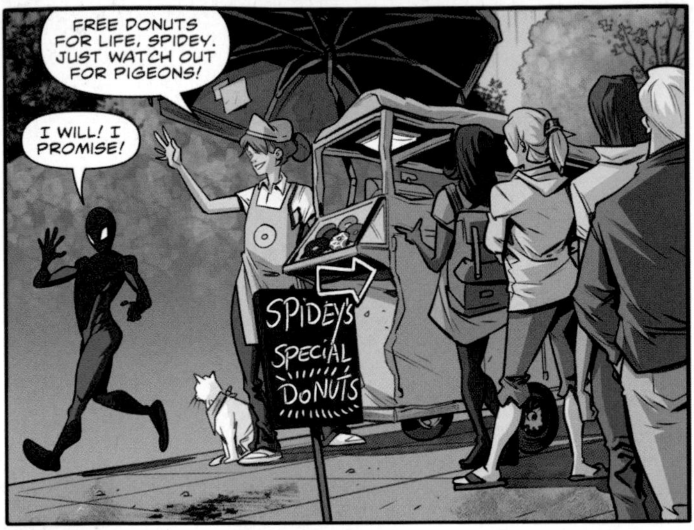
FREE DONUTS FOR LIFE, SPIDEY. JUST WATCH OUT FOR PIGEONS!
I WILL! I PROMISE!
SPIDEY'S SPECIAL DONUTS
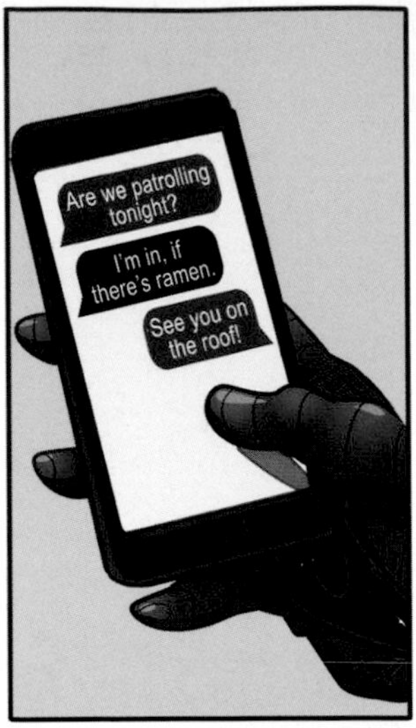
Are we patrolling tonight?
I'm in, if there's ramen.
See you on the roof!
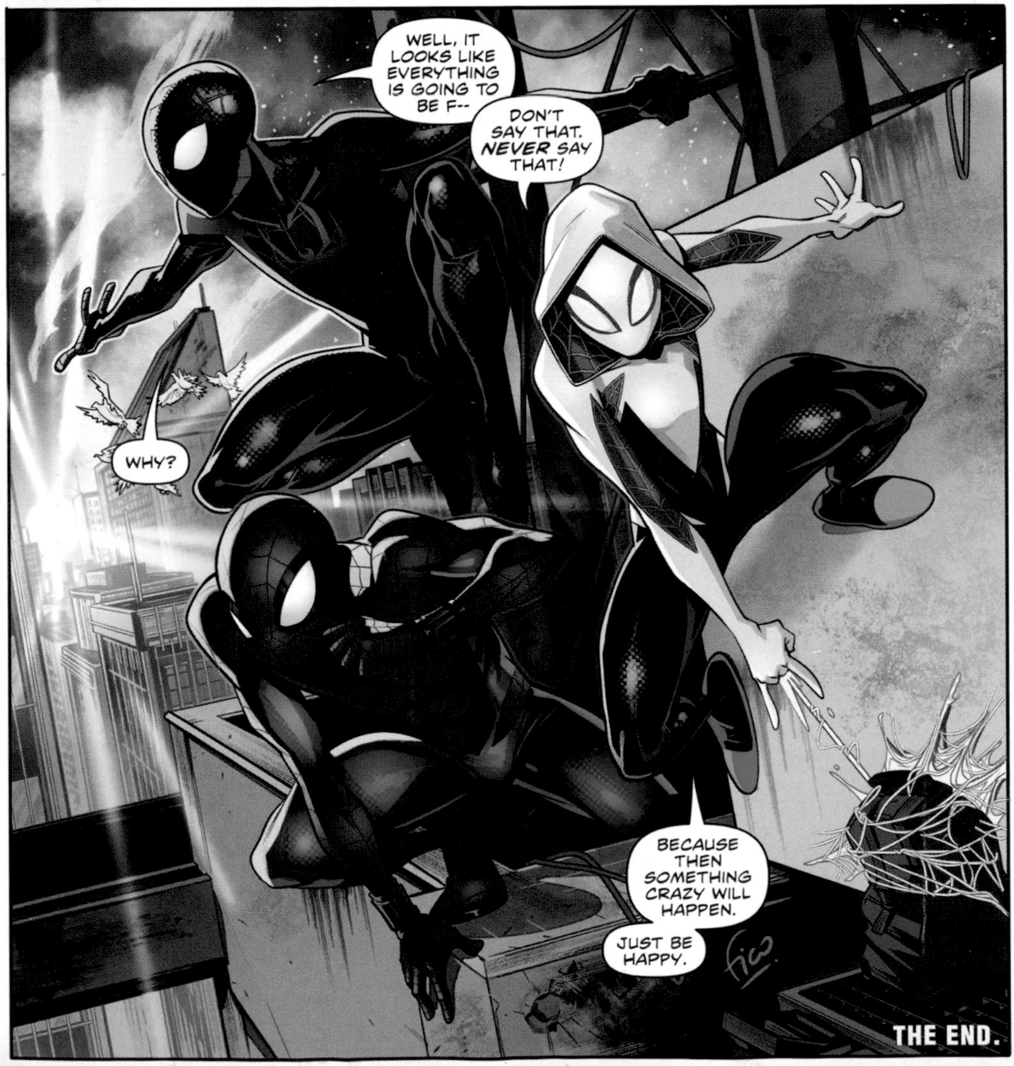
WELL, IT LOOKS LIKE EVERYTHING IS GOING TO BE F--
DON'T SAY THAT. NEVER SAY THAT!
WHY?
BECAUSE THEN SOMETHING CRAZY WILL HAPPEN.
JUST BE HAPPY.
THE END.

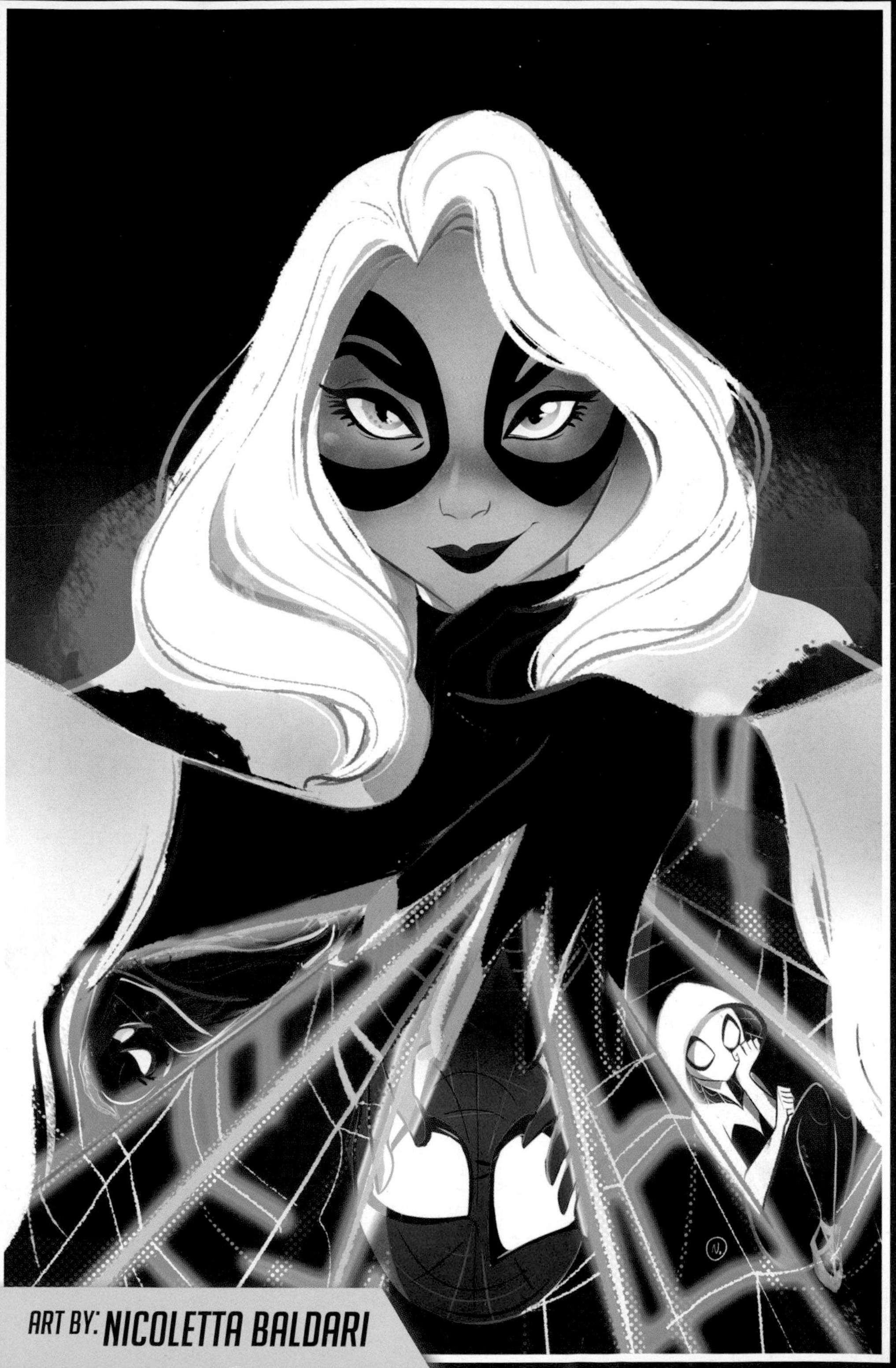

ART BY: NICOLETTA BALDARI

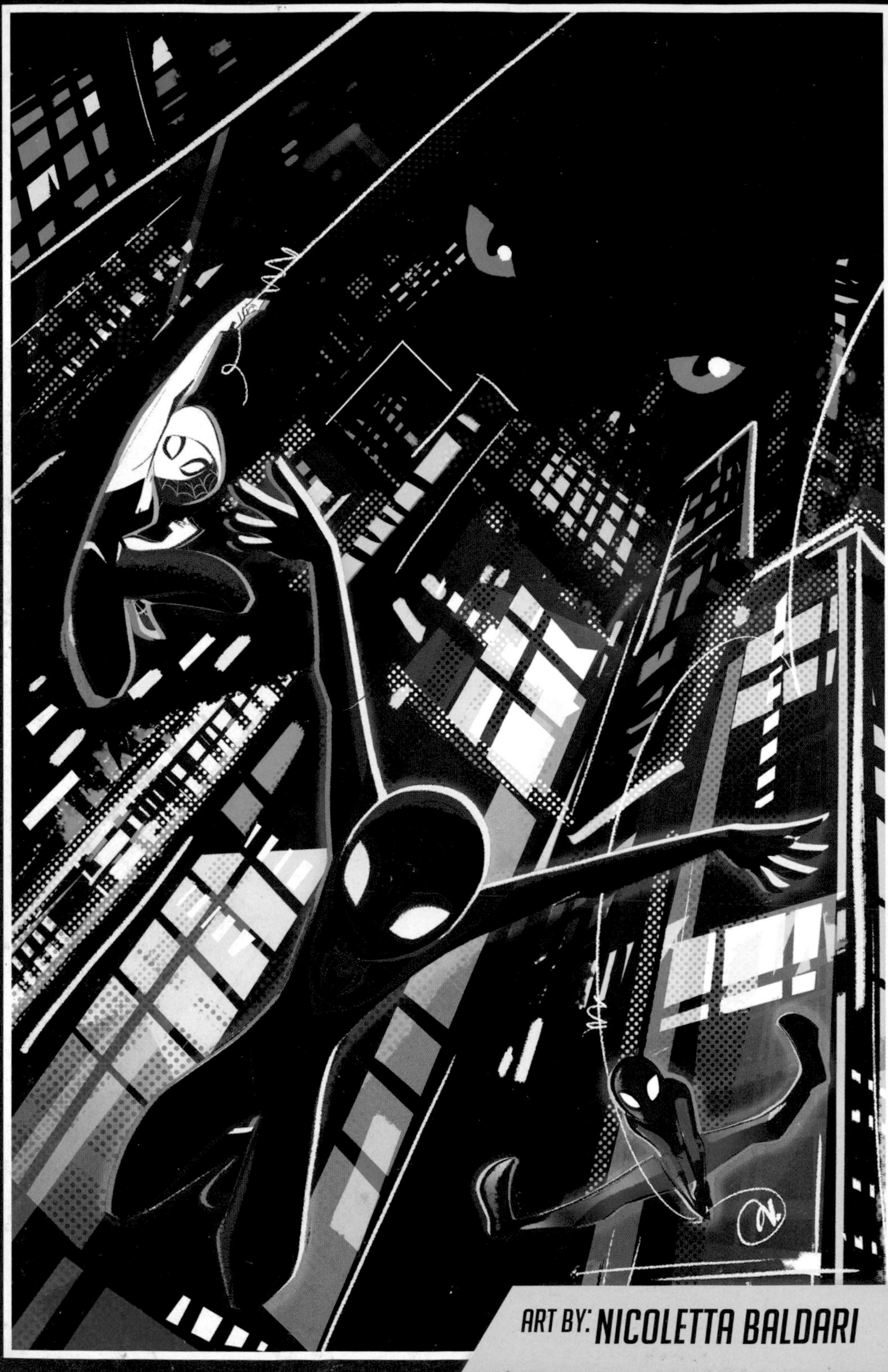

ART BY: NICOLETTA BALDARI